Old Moon

Volume VI

Published by Old Moon Quarterly.

Each author retains the copyright to their story.

Cover art by Senkai Yami
(https://www.instagram.com/senkai_yami/)

The collection and arrangement © 2023 by Julian Barona.

Contents

Introduction

Dear Reader,

The dead walk.

Not, perhaps, outside your window, nor even in that unlighted and mutual crypt we term our Earth. Rather, they walk within you, dear reader. And within me—within, indeed, all of us who can (by deed and inclination) claim the title "reader." The dead inhabit us: their words, their deeds, the ghosts of their philosophies, the phantoms of their loves and their hates. That is the magic of reading—it makes necromancers us of all, for by reading the words of the dead, we revive in ourselves their work and their life.

Is it any wonder, then, that authors find themselves continually attracted to the graveyard's rich and fruitful loam? Fantasy fiction, and sword-and-sorcery fiction in particular, grub up the corpses of the dead as foe and friend alike. Some of us may recall (sometimes with that sneer born of over-familiarity) the zombie apocalypse craze of the early 2000s, but the history of the fantastic dead claws for itself a deeper and more storied lineage. Indeed, some of the most popular fantasy works of recent and popular imagination deal prominently with the unquiet dead: the Vampire Counts of *Warhammer* and the Scourge of *Warcraft*; the unmemoried hollows of *Dark Souls* and its offshoots; the innumerable striga, rotfiends, botchlings, wraiths and so on of the *Witcher*. One need not stray too far nor too deep into the history of literature to see examples there as well: the Ringwraiths and Barrow-wights of Tolkien's legendarium, the ghouls of Lovecraft and Smith, the undead "howe-dweller" faced by Grettir in his eponymous saga, and more besides.

Often in these stories, the dead constitute our hero's foe. One might read into this some interesting symbolism, were one inclined towards such literary horologies—by slaying the mouldered, ambulatory corpse, does the hero (in some way) conquer that personified Death who, like a specter itself, looms over all human endeavor? Perhaps, perhaps. Or maybe it is just good fun to imagine something so grimy—so gribbly—as a walking corpse! And even more fun to imagine it struck down by sword-blow or spell-blast. The truth may lie (as it so often does) somewhere between these two poles. Or even outside their remit entire.

But whatever the reason, the dead endure, both in our imaginations and in our stories. At *Old Moon Quarterly*, we keep our spade in, as it were. We upshovel the dead, and we honor them. Or, occasionally, smack them with an axe. The dead, we think, appreciate it. Certainly, we appreciate them.

We must appreciate them, given the stories we're publishing in this issue, for the dead figure in them prominently. We begin, in fact, with a story in the best Smithian mode: Josh Reynolds's "The Orphan of Bones," where certain acolytes of Mordiggian must return to their god's embrace one of his own children. That the child is dead does not, of course, dissuade our protagonists (nor does it diminish their hunger).

The lines between life, death and dream blur in this volume's second story, R.L. Summerling's "Corpse Wax," wherein a swordswoman learns that beheading the tyrant-king does not always end tyranny itself.

Neither of our poems this issue—Katherine Quevedo's "What They Don't Tell You about Training To Slay" and R.H. Berry's "Respite"—deal expressly with the dead, risen or otherwise, but they certainly provide different looks at aspects of the fantasy-adventure story: the trauma inherited by many of the warrior-heroes we so love in the former case, and the delightfully seductive and comforting nature of certain dangerous beasts (human and otherwise) in the latter.

Veteran sword-and-sorcery author Dariel R. A. Quiogue's "Marchers in the Fog" refracts the ghoulish themes of Reynolds's story, albeit through the mirror of the 17th century European Wars of Religion. The dead themselves do not figure in the story as characters themselves, but perhaps one might say the protagonist (by the story's end) is himself a sort of corpse, at least spiritually and morally.

Our concluding stories, the E.R. Eddison-esque "The Festering Mantle," written by J.M. Hayes, and the extraordinarily stylized "Diary of the Wolf" by Adam McPhee, admittedly break from the theme of the dead (or dead-eaters, as it were) which typify this issue's earlier stories. However, each story owes its clearest inspiration to authors who themselves number among the unnumbered dead we mentioned at the top of this essay—Eddison, aforementioned, and (intriguingly) Samuel Pepys, respectively. They are not pastiches of said authors' work, but reimagine elements of them and refashion them into something both wholly unique, yet in dialogue with these past works.

And is that not the work of all authors? Of all artists, even? None of us (or rather, very few) draw our inspiration from works created solely within living memory. No, we call up the dead and (like Shelley's good doctor) stitch them to other parts and, with the thunder of our imaginations, galvanize them into new (un)life. But the dead do not rise alone. Neither Eddison nor Pepys (nor any author) wrote in a vacuum. When we uncask them, they bring with them their own influences and the shades of their influences, and so we perceive (like shadows on a wall) the chain of the everlasting dead, stretching back and back and back from the screens of our e-readers and our laptops into the lantern-lit rooms of epochs past and back further yet, perhaps nigh unto that cavern whence we all once sprung, where the first hominid storytellers, voices shy with the novelty of their tongues, first called from the earth their own dead, their own stories.

So join us, dear readers, as we engage in that grand and human tradition. Join us, fellow necromancers. The dead are waiting.

The Editors at Old Moon

The Orphan of Bones

By Josh Reynolds

Amina Algol stepped lightly and swiftly across the sandy stones, her bare feet making no sound. She flitted from shadow to shadow, following the line of half-toppled pillars through the ruins, towards the distant flicker of firelight.

Above her, slinking along the broken tops of the pillars, Bera, her sister, easily kept pace. Then, four legs were swifter than two. Unless, of course, those four belonged to one as heavy as her brother. She glanced to her right and spotted him instantly, though her eyes were weak as any human's.

Arif galumphed across the broken ground with simian simplicity, his passage loud to her ears, utterly lacking in Bera's cat-like dignity. She shook her head, and hoped that their prey would not hear him and take fright.

She sprang over a fallen statue, and slid to a stop. The campfire burned steadily, a triangle of light at the other end of the avenue. The ruins were not large—a minor trading town, humbled during some ancient cataclysm, and left to the sands. But there was a well, and a cistern of rainwater. An ideal place to camp for two men travelling through the desert.

She sank into a crouch and crept towards the light, one hand on the hilt of her sword. She stopped in the shelter of a cracke plinth and sank to her haunches, eyes narrowed. A moment later, Bera joined her. Her sister dropped lightly onto the plinth, eyes gleaming. "I can smell them from here," she growled.

Amina glanced up. Her sister was lithe and deadly, with a square skull and jaws that could crack even the thickest bones. She gripped the edges of the plinth with claws strong enough to peel open stone sarcophagi. Bera leaned down and nuzzled her. "Shall we share them with Arif, sister, or shall we leave the greedyguts to hunt his own prey?"

"You would not do that, sister," Arif growled, as he crept towards them, head low. In contrast to their sister, he was bulky with muscle and marrow. But like her, he was shaggy and mouldy after the current fashion, with mottled flesh and thick, hyena-like jaws set into his handsome, sloped skull.

The two were the very flower of ghoulish kind. Amina, however, was a blossom of a different sort. Where they were great and powerful, she was small and dark and lacking even the smallest patch of mould on her skin. The runt of the litter.

Her high, proud features resembled those of a woman of distant Khem, or so she'd been told, with thick black hair bound back in tight, wormlike braids. Lacking a proper ghoulish hide, she instead wore a banded cuirass, scavenged from a battlefield, and clothes made from zoog-hide. She wore neither gloves nor boots, her palms and soles toughened by a childhood spent among the lightless depths of Pnath.

Arif leaned heavily against Amina, his comforting stink enveloping her. "You would not leave me to starve, sister," he whined. "What would mother say?"

Bera glared down at him. "Mother would say that you are fat enough already. Missing a meal or six will not do you any ill."

"You would see me wither away." He nudged Amina with his shaggy head. "Tell her, sister. Tell her how I will wither from such neglect."

Amina sighed and scratched behind his pointed ear. "Quiet, brother. They will hear."

"They will hear his belly rumbling, is what they'll hear," Bera murmured.

"What does it matter?" Arif said. "There are but two of them, and they are only men. Let us fall on them, and suck the marrow from their bones."

"They might be wizards," Bera said. "Only wizards are foolish enough to cross the Bnazic Desert, and plunder the forgotten cities of Khem."

"Or merchants," Arif said. "They look like merchants."

"Maybe they are sailors," Amina said. "It does not matter. They have the child, and we must get him back."

"Poor mite," Bera growled, sadly. "He must be frightened."

"He is the son of kings," said Arif. "And he knows we will come. What is there to be frightened of?"

"Many things," Amina said. "They would not have survived this long, if they were not formidable. Even if it is only the pair, we must show caution." She peered at the campfire, wondering at the nature of those who defiled such places of antiquity. It was not uncommon, sadly. The desert was full of adventurers' bones, as were the ruins which dotted the sands. But some rare few were dogged enough to survive.

Ghouls had watched and wagered as these two had crept through lightless catacombs, seeking forgotten treasures. The expectation was that some trap or beast would claim their lives, leaving their flesh for Mordiggian's children. But, as was sometimes the case, death had not made an appearance, and bellies had stayed empty.

And then they'd found the prince's chamber, and any amusement the ghouls might have felt evaporated. Howls of rage and despair had echoed through the nighted vaults of the city as the pair made their way back to the surface. Messengers had flown swiftly to the priests of Mordiggian in Khem and Meroe, seeking the aid of seasoned hunters. And thus, Amina and her siblings had been dispatched to pursue the pair across the desert.

It had taken them no more than a day to find the trail, but their quarry, atop camels, moved swiftly over the sea of sand. They had shadowed them from one oasis to the next, burrowing into the sand during the day, and loping across the dunes by night. And now, at last, she and her siblings had caught up with them. And with their prisoner.

She frowned. The prince was but a boy, and an orphan at that. His parents had passed on, and now resided elsewhere—perhaps even in the waking world, as some had whispered. Whatever their fate, the boy had been left here in the Dreamlands, and in the care of her folk. That he had been dead longer than she had been alive was of no matter. For a ghoul, responsibility did not end with life's leaving.

Arif grunted. "I grow hungry."

Bera looked at him. "That comes as no surprise." He made to snarl at her, but Amina caught his snout in her hand, silencing him.

"Hush, brother." Amina looked at her sister. "I will go first. Follow my lead."

Bera eyed her uncertainly. "It is too dangerous."

Amina shrugged. "While I distract them, you two can circle around."

"You take too many chances, sister."

"Someone must." Amina scratched Bera's chin. "Do not fear, sister. I have no interest in meeting Mordiggian just yet."

"If you die, can I eat your belly-meats?" Arif said, tongue lolling.

"No, I will eat them," Bera said.

"Why should you get them?"

"I love her more."

"You may share them," Amina said, ending the argument before it could really begin. However, she smiled as she said it, pleased by the show of affection. "Now hush." She rose to her feet and started down the avenue, moving lightly. She heard Bera and Arif split up, one to either side of her.

It was an old trick, perfected in the bone-fields of Pnath during ghast-hunts. Their skill in such endeavors was one of the reasons they had been selected by the priests of Mordiggian to act as the god's hand in earthly matters. Few ghouls could match a ghast, and fewer still had successfully hunted one. Usually it was the other way around.

"I will give them the chance to return the prince," Amina whispered, as she walked. "It is only just." She could not say why the thought had occurred to her.

"Mercy, sister?" Bera asked. "You know such a thing cannot be."

"And why not? Mordiggian is a just god."

"But wrathful, sister. When he demands recompense, it is best to offer it up without much argument." Bera snuffled at her side. "They stole from us, and must be punished."

Amina nodded, but did not reply. The firelight swelled, and she heard the murmur of voices, and the grumbling of camels. They made a tidy camp, these thieves. They'd chosen what might once have been a hostelry, though it had long since succumbed to time's edge. Two broken walls kept the wind at bay, and the camels had been hitched to the remains of the entryway. She crept closer, moving stealthily. Bera and Arif padded nearby in silence.

"No guards," Arif muttered.

"They are foolish," Bera said.

"Or confident," Amina said. This close, she could see that the campfire burned merrily at the center of the camp, set in the old hearth-pit, and the two thieves sat to either side of it, jesting with one another as they took turns stirring a bubbling iron pot hung from the cooking spit.

The smell of whatever they were cooking made her stomach burble. She'd often indulged in human food, when her siblings weren't around to mock her for it. It was an illicit vice, shameful and invigorating all at once. She sniffed the air, enjoying the tang of unfamiliar spices, as she weaved her way through the camels.

The animals groaned as they caught the ghouls' scent, and thumped the ground with their feet. She stroked one's neck as she passed, causing it to rear and paw the air. The bells on its saddle clanked, and the men shot to their feet, hands on their weapons.

"Who's there?" one barked. A harsh accent, as of Baharna or one of the other kingdoms that hugged the coast of Oriab.

"A traveller," she called out.

"And why are you creeping among our camels?" the other said. A smooth voice. Like that of a man of Serranian, which hung in the clouds far to the west.

"Might I share your fire?"

"Come closer, and we shall see."

She gestured silently to her siblings, and they slunk out of sight, circling through the shadows. She stepped into the light, one hand on her sword. The smooth-voiced man whistled softly as he peered at her. He was dressed colorfully beneath a battered hauberk, and his face was unscarred and pale. His hands were crossed atop the jasper pommel of the sword sheathed on his hip, and he stood at ease.

Beside him, his companion was much less relaxed. A short, pugnacious-looking man, with a face that had seen the wrong end of many a blow, wearing stained travel leathers beneath a cloak of zebra-hide.

"And who might you be, fair lady?" the smooth-voiced man said.

"You first," Amina said.

The man smiled. "Geull. And my friend here is Stayl."

"Don't tell her my name," Stayl protested. "She might be some desert spirit, come to snatch our souls from our sleeping bodies!"

"We're not asleep," Geull pointed out.

"Even so," Stayl said. He looked at Amina. "Now you—are you a spirit?"

"No." Amina smiled, careful not to show her teeth. She had filed them, to better fit in with her family. Stayl looked at Geull.

"I don't believe her."

Geull rolled his eyes. "Your name, please."

"Amina." Past the fire, she saw a collection of packs and saddlebags. And among them, the prince. The sarcophagus was small, as befitted one who had not reached his tenth mortal year, and its once-rich hues had faded, and the royal gilt adorning its facing had tarnished. She felt a pang of sympathy for the little prince. An orphan, taken from the only home he'd ever known, and carted across the desert like so much plunder.

"A lovely name." Geull frowned. "Not one I've heard before, though. Khemish?"

"It is the name my father gave me," she said. "It means 'charnel blossom' in the meepery of our people."

"Meepery?" Stayl muttered. He and Geull traded glances. Geull shrugged.

"Come then, my lady. Sit and warm yourself before our fire, if you would."

As she sat, she saw them both glance at her feet. She wondered if they were checking her for cloven hooves. She smiled. Gossip to the contrary, only a few of her folk had such things. Geull ladled out a bowlful of stew and proffered it to her. "You must be hungry. No pack, no supplies. No mount, even." He paused. "Unless you left it somewhere safe?"

After the briefest of hesitations, she nodded. "Safe, yes."

Again, the two men traded glances. She let no sign of the chagrin she felt show on her face. Geull continued to proffer the stew. Gingerly, she took it, reasoning that to do otherwise would elicit even more suspicion. It smelled good, but she did not eat. Ghouls ate together, or not at all. At least when within sight of each other.

If her hosts noticed, they gave no sign. They tucked in with gusto, as she watched, interested. It was rare that she had the opportunity to study men in such close proximity. Normally, there was much screaming and wailing. This sort of companionable silence was odd, to her. She watched them eat, and listened to them laugh, and found them not so different to her own folk. And yet, they were nonetheless utterly alien in their manner.

Sometimes, she wondered why her father had decided to spare her, given the gulf between them. What had he made of that squalling infant, slick with blood and left to die on a battlefield? Had he considered eating her there and then, as Arif often joked?

The thought did not upset her. To eat and be eaten was the way of things. Ghouls ate the flesh of the dead, whatever the nature of the corpse. It was a high honour to be devoured by your kin on your day of passing. Flesh stripped, bones cracked, marrow sucked—all of it helped speed the soul to the charnel gardens of

Mordiggian, where the burying grounds stretched forever, and no casket was sealed with lead.

"You never did say where you were from," Geull said, startling her slightly.

"Khem," she said, which might well be the truth.

"Really? I've heard it is quite lovely, this time of year."

"Yes." She nodded, though she had no idea. Geull smiled, and she wondered if he suspected. He glanced at her bowl.

"Stew not to your taste?"

"Maybe she already ate," Stayl said. "Is that it, then? Did you have a meal out there, with no pack and no mount, by yourself in the sands?"

Amina set her bowl aside. "Perhaps I am simply not hungry."

"And not thirsty, either. You have not asked to share our water. The desert is dark, and cold, but you wear neither boots nor cloak."

She made a show of warming her hands. "The fire is adequate." Beyond the glare of the light, she could make out a darker patch of shadow, slithering low across the broken walls of the hostelry. Bera, getting into position.

"Someone has been following us," Stayl said, ladling more stew into his bowl.

"Flattered as we are, we must ask why," Geull added, setting aside his own bowl. "Not our good looks, I assume."

Amina paused, considering the question. She could sense this hunt nearing its end. They were wary, but did not yet realize their danger. Once they did, it would come down to fangs and claws, as it always did. She felt a moment's regret as she considered it. Sometimes, she thought that she ought to go among men more often, to learn their ways better. But, then, was the ghoulish way not the best of all ways? Nonetheless, the thought lingered.

"Why did you take him?" she said, ignoring Geull's question.

"Him?" Geull said. She nodded to the sarcophagus, sitting among the packs. He glanced at it, and then back at her, his expression curious.

"Is it a him, then? And how do you know?"

Stayl stirred the stew. "She's a witch, obviously. Only a witch would wander the desert with no boots. And who is she to ask us our business?"

Amina ignored him, and studied Geull. He was handsome, in the way some mortals were. Too, there was a certain ghoulishness to the way he moved—all at ease, and untroubled by the world around him. He seemed equally interested in her, and his eyes roamed freely. She caught his eyes, and he grinned ruefully. "My apologies, but you are striking."

Stayl snorted. Amina glanced at him, and then back at Geull. He was grinning now, and there was something that might have been invitation in his expression. She looked at the sarcophagus. "Why did you seek him out?" she asked, again.

Geull frowned. "We didn't, really. We came looking for treasures—gold, silver, precious jewels and the like. They say the wealth of ages lies hidden beneath these sands, ripe for the taking."

"They say," Stayl snorted.

"But you found none of that."

"No. Nothing of any value, save that." He looked at the sarcophagus. "There are wizards and scholars aplenty in Carcassonne and Oonai who will pay for such relics. Too, the dust of mummies is quite prized by the perfumers of Sinara. It seemed a waste to leave it."

"Him," Amina corrected, gently. Geull inclined his head.

"Him."

"And we found little else of value, down there. Certainly not enough to justify risking our necks in this wasteland." Stayl cast a baleful eye at his companion. "This is the ruby eye of Hlem all over again."

"The jungle wasn't that bad."

"I was nearly eaten by a snake the size of an elephant."

"Nearly being the operative term." Geull smiled widely at Amina. "Would you like to hear the story?"

"She wouldn't," Stayl said.

"She might."

"I don't," Amina said.

"See?" Stayl said. He peered at her. "How many?"

She paused. "How many what?"

"How many of you are there?" Geull looked around. "We are not deaf, and someone's stomach has been rumbling the entire time we've been talking." He smiled. "Bandits, then?"

"Not bandits," Amina said sharply, somewhat insulted by the idea, as well as annoyed by Arif's blunder. "If anyone is a bandit here, it is the pair of you. Thieves and looters."

"Thieves?" Geull said.

"Looters?" Stayl said.

"Seekers of fortune, I'd say," Geull looked at his companion. "Adventurers, even, but hardly thieves."

"Not at the moment, at least," Stayl said. He looked around. "I heard something."

Geull nodded. "Yes. How many of you, then?"

Amina ignored the question. "Whatever you call yourselves, the deed is done. I've come to ask you to release your prisoner."

"Prisoner?" Geull said, startled. "What prisoner?"

"Him." Amina pointed again at the tiny sarcophagus, with its faded colors.

"That's not a him, that's an it," Stayl said. "Tomb-leavings, is all, like I said."

Amina frowned. "You have taken him from his home. He was left in the keeping of my folk by his parents."

"He's dead," Stayl said, as if to a child.

Amina nodded. "And has been for ten centuries. Yet he is in our keeping nonetheless. Release him, and you will be forgiven your trespasses."

Geull laughed. "Trespasses? What offense have we given, my lady? A ruin is public property, at least in the eyes of sensible folk."

Stayl glared at her, and tapped the hilt of his blade. He rose slowly, eyes never leaving her face. "Geull, stop playing coy. You know as well as I that this is the one who's been following us."

Geull glanced at his companion. "Is that so?" His smile widened. "Have you been following us, Lady Amina?"

She said nothing. Stayl took a step towards her.

Out in the dark, Bera snarled softly. Stayl tensed, alert. "She's definitely not alone."

"I did not say that I was."

"Would your companions like some stew?" Geull said. His voice was mild, but his expression was wary. They were not fools, these two. Fools would have left their bones bleaching beneath the desert sun already. But they were more dangerous than she'd thought. Perhaps they had faced worse things than ghouls in the night.

"They do not care for stew," she said. "They prefer...heartier fare."

The two men exchanged glances. "Ah," Geull said, after a moment. "Then would you be amenable to a cut of the profits? Say...twenty percent?"

Stayl made a choking sound. "Twenty percent?"

Geull glanced at him. "A small price to pay, I think."

"We should pay nothing. We braved the dangers of the tomb, and the trek across the trackless sands. What has she done, save follow us and make vague threats?"

"I have not threatened you," Amina said. "Had I done so, you would know." She gestured sharply. Somewhere to her left, Arif snarled. The sound bounced among the ruins, swelling to fill the air.

Stayl turned. "What was that?"

"My brother," Amina said.

Bera growled low and long, from her right.

"And that?" Geull said.

"My sister."

The two men looked at one another. "Three to two," Geull said, as he climbed to his feet, shaking his head in what might have been disappointment.

"Unfortunate odds," Stayl grunted. He looked at her, eyes hot with anger. "She was a distraction, I expect." He turned his glare on Geull. "And not the first time a pretty face has done so, in regards to you, Geull."

"I am but a man, Stayl."

"And a fool."

"They go hand in hand, I find," Amina said. She rose to her feet, ready to leap back and draw her blade, if it came to it. Stayl looked as if he might attack at any moment.

Geull laughed lightly. "Indeed. Much to my chagrin, that is the case." He glanced at the sarcophagus. "Speaking of cases...that one is worth a king's ransom to us."

"Is it worth your lives?" Amina caught the glint of Bera's eyes from atop the wall behind the two men. She could not see Arif, but she knew that he was close.

Geull sighed. "Sadly, yes."

Before she could react, he had his sword out, and had used it to wrench the stewpot from its place above the fire. Whirling about, he flung the bubbling pot full at Bera, who yelped and sprang out of sight. At the same moment, Stayl lunged, blade angled for a killing thrust. Amina dodged the blow, but only just, and Stayl spun, quick as a cat.

Amina tore her blade from its sheath and intercepted his next blow. They reeled back and forth, trading sword-strokes. Amina had learned her art the hard way, but Stayl was far more skilled. It was all she could do to keep him at bay. She heard Arif howl from somewhere nearby, and saw a blur of mottled color as he bounded towards the swordsman. Stayl turned and cursed, his blade flickering. Arif gave a strangled bark and scrambled back, out of reach of the blade.

"Corpse-eaters," Stayl spat.

"Better that than thieves," Amina said. She cut at him, but he parried the blow. Stayl backed towards the light, keeping them both in sight.

"Geull," he called out. "Get the packs."

"Gotten and going," Geull called out. "They're between us and the camels."

"Then we'll move them."

Arif growled low in his throat. "Not likely." He paced into the light of the fire, and Stayl hissed in revulsion.

Geull looked at Amina as she stepped to Arif's side. "You must take after your mother," he said, with forced cheerfulness. He'd dragged several of the packs and the sarcophagus to the fire, for ease of carrying

Amina smiled, showing her teeth. "This can end now." She levelled her blade. "Release the prince, and you will be forgiven."

In reply, Geull snatched a brand from the fire and swung it about. Arif drew back instinctively, and Geull stamped forward, blade hissing out. Amina caught it with her own, and saw Stayl dart for the camels. "Arif," she shouted.

Arif swept past her, and bounded towards Stayl, jaws wide. As the latter turned, blade raised, Bera lunged from behind him, steaming gobbets of stew staining her fur. She struck the man like a bullet launched from a sling, and Amina heard bones break from the impact.

Geull shouted wordlessly as his companion went down beneath the weight of Amina's siblings. He drove Amina back, turned and leapt for the sarcophagus. Amina followed him, but stopped as he chopped it open with a single, wild blow. Grabbing a handful of mouldering linen, he wrenched the prince from his bed in a gout of dust.

"Leave him," he roared. "Leave him, or I cast this bundle of bones in to the fire!"

Arif and Bera stopped at Amina's shout, and turned bloody muzzles towards Geull. Stayl was groaning, but still alive. She lowered her sword. "Release him," she said. "He has done nothing to you."

"He is dead. I am alive, and intend to stay that way. Stayl—do you live?"

Stayl groaned again. Geull grimaced. "Good enough." He looked at Amina. "If we return this thing, you will leave us in peace?"

"You will be forgiven," she said. Her hand edged towards the knife thrust through her belt. If Geull noticed, he gave no sign.

He set the prince down. "Then I humbly beseech forgiveness." He stepped back, hands spread. "Stayl...?"

"I...gods...I beseech forgiveness," the other man groaned.

Amina stepped back. At her gesture, Arif and Bera backed away, growling. Geull frowned and moved to aid his companion. He glanced at her as he passed. "A shame, my lady. Perhaps we'll meet again, under more salubrious circumstances."

Amina didn't reply. She watched as he bent to help the injured man to his feet. When his back was to her, she met Bera's yellow gaze and nodded. Then, she drew her knife and threw it with a single, smooth motion. The blade caught Geull in the shoulder, and he cried out. He turned, and she lunged, driving her sword past his and into his gut. Her momentum carried Geull back, against the wall. He goggled at her as she leaned her weight against the pommel, sawing the sword into him.

Behind her, Arif and Bera fell on the gawping Stayl, jaws wide. His screams spiralled up and up, until they passed the point of audibility. Geull clutched at her hands, trying to push her back. "But—you said..." he gurgled.

"That you would be forgiven. And you have been." She spoke softly. Soothingly. "But still, you must pay the price. Mordiggian is a just god, but wrathful. And we are very hungry." She twisted the blade, and his heels beat on the sands for a moment. Then, with a sigh, he slumped. She tore the sword loose, and turned.

Bera looked up, strands of meat and muscle hanging from her jaws. She nudged Arif, and he tore a chunk of Stayl loose and offered it up. "Come, sister," Bera said. "You have earned it."

"Eat what you like. There is plenty for all."

"Not for long," Arif grunted around a mouthful.

Shaking her head, Amina sheathed her sword, and went to the prince. His little form was naught but bones now, swaddled in linen vestments. Carefully, she placed him back in his sarcophagus and closed it. He would be returned to his home, and the care of those who knew him best. An orphan, perhaps, but not unloved.

Almost idly, she picked up her forgotten bowl of stew and dipped in a bloody finger.

It really was quite good.

Corpse Wax

By R.L. Summerling

At dawn, still gripping the bloodied hilt of Wetgullet and stinking of war, you ask to be brought to St. Lillians. The city is a luminous ribcage, needle-thin towers puncturing crisp skies. Nascent sunlight drips honey over spires. These are the precious, feral days in between the imperial tyrants of old and whatever is to follow. Change is here. As the saying goes, *a child of Vardanel cannot be unborn.*

Only now, in this holy enclave of the city, has the tension finally begun to abate. The pain of fresh wounds forces you to your knees at the altar. You sink toward the floor and place palms flat against ancient stone and weep. The Owd Scriven chants his blessing as he weaves gold through the air. He has worn the same scat-coloured robes, the same vulpine leather mask, as long as you can remember. You try to focus on his words, to celebrate this moment, but even now you are haunted by the tongueless presence of your oldest enemy. The severed head of Menas Glas, speared on your son's pike, watches you. It cannot be so, he is dead as the saints, yet you will not let the head out of your sight. It would not be beyond the last king of Vardenel to reveal a parlor trick. He may be alive yet.

Only your two children accompanied you to the altar, the rest of the army—so depleted in number it is hard to call them one still—wait outside. Arabella kneels by you in solidarity. She holds her shoulder, hastily bandaged between leaving the battlefield and reentering the city. Buccio stands guard by the door; even now, he watches for assassins. You suckled them as babes and now they are grown into warriors, more skilled and shrewd than you. They have learned how to be ruthless, to their advantage. But did you show them enough love? Instill in them enough compassion to rule without tyranny? Some days you look into their flint-grey eyes and wonder.

The Owd Scriven blows out the ceremonial candles and helps Arabella lift you to your feet. "It is done," he says.

You step outside, and the vicious spring sunshine stings your eyes. You cannot be sure how long you have been awake. Buccio notes how the weather exalts you. Even the air is redolent of victory. Oh, how the bells ring out over Vardanel as jubilant morning light rains over the city. You were named Clara for the bells; their song, so bright on the day of your birth, would always remind your parents of their only daughter.

One of the guards passes you a skin of water and a hard wheaten cake, which you swiftly toss to the red-breasted linnets. The birds perched in the surrounding rowan trees sing, for they know. Menas Glas is dead and you cannot eat. You swung Wetgullet at the king's neck and his head rolled into the dark forested night. It had been the will of the people and you acted upon it. Five long years of war, many dead on both sides. But it is over and whatever happens next is out of your hands. Many of the men propose finding a nearby tavern in order to begin the celebrations, but you simply ask to be taken to the little house on Copeland Street where Arabella and Buccio were born. The room where the embers of rebellion were first lit. The bed on which you watched Mateo transition from this life to the next. You cannot call it a home, you have not rested there in so long.

Arabella looks to Buccio, a conversation between them conducted in silence. They close in around you so the others would not hear. Buccio, still bearing the speared head, brings Menas Glas as if he were a fourth in your circle of confidence.

"The council will be waiting on your guidance, Mother. They will expect you to name a leader. They will anticipate you nominating yourself and that you will have an actionable plan in place to secure the city. There is much work to be done," Arabella says.

"I'm too old to politic," you say. "It should be either of you, or Agapeto if neither of you want it."

They look at you as if they were babes again, waiting for you to divide a handful of raspberries between them. Their concerns seem so insignificant. You have played your part in the history of this city. The burden of what happens next cannot be on your shoulders.

"But, it is your time Mother," Buccio says, softly.

"It is time for me to go home, children," you say, taking the speared head from Buccio and asking one of the guards to bring a carriage.

A guard has left a small pack of your belongings by the blackthorn tree. You have few possessions. A journal, a ring extracted from the stiff hand of Iones, your beloved lieutenant. You bend down to pick up the satchel and suddenly the world pitches. You sense movement overhead and your battle reflexes, still sharp, kick into action. But as you look to the sky, you see no falling arrows. Something strange has occurred. The sun has divided, there are now two glowing orbs in the sky. Iridescent circles float across your vision and a curtain of darkness begins to move across the sky. Knees buckle. Buccio's tall frame rushes to protect you. A low rumbling noise, ceaseless thunder smothers everything. You cannot hear what anyone says.

* * *

In the little house on Copeland Street, you tell Buccio and Arabella that they must go out and celebrate. You're fine, just exhausted. They deliberate in hushed tones in the parlor. In order to solidify their position, they need to be seen. To remind the people which family brought them victory. But their concern for you is palpable.

"Children, I insist you go. Nothing will be achieved by watching me sleep."

* * *

The unnatural quiet of an empty house at night. Sleep will not come. Abstract shapes cobweb across your vision, forming strange, unnatural constellations. You are tired to your bones, yet as soon as sleep comes you are transported to that moment on the hill. A hatred for this house blazes through you. You never felt haunted like this on the road. You were never alone like this when you were with your troops, when a sleepless night meant shots of plum liquor and sharing stories underneath the stars.

In the corner of your chamber, the rotting head of your oldest enemy stands. Long hair dark as ink. His skin belies wealth; even in death, he looks regal. You look at his pallid lips and wonder how many people that mouth has caressed. You would kiss him now, bite into him like a ripe pear, just so you could say you stole the final embrace from the last king of Vardanel. Maybe it's just the flickering light of the fire, but you swear you see his lips move. You pull the rough blanket around you. A low murmuring emits from Menas Glas. Some symptom of rigor mortis surely. The murmuring grows louder and fear seizes your throat. And that's when you realize he is laughing. The old bastard is laughing at you. His laughter turns into hysterics and you scream for his silence. A terracotta jug on your bedside table shatters. Water seeps through the cracks in the floor.

* * *

Arabella and Buccio did not return home before dawn. They clattered around with an inebriated illusion of stealth. You rouse them at noon, their eyes bleary, faces slow with sleep. Arabella bleeds through her bandages.

"Children, there is something I need your help with. You must return to Fairman's Copse, where we piled the bodies of the king's army. You must locate the body of Menas Glas and from his skin, scrape the corpse wax and bring it to me. The sun is high, but it is not yet too hot."

"But why Mother?" Buccio asks

"Because I believe there is some lingering malevolence that can only be extinguished with fire."

"Keeping the head of Menas Glas here isn't good for you."

"You will be rid of it soon, Mother. The Liberation parade is tomorrow. You must present the head to the people, it belongs to them." Arabella says. Buccio nods.

"Do you always agree with each other?" you smirk. They had begun to speak so alike, it was getting difficult to tell them apart. Arabella was once shy and moved with the lyricism of a seer. Buccio would have done anything to earn his mother's approval, his voice loud and clear and always demanding. They bore an acerbic hatred for each other you worried they would never overcome. There were always tears over some stolen iced bun or a destroyed doll or the perception of preferential treatment administered to one or the other. Constant snipping at each that you did not have the experience to understand was completely natural between siblings, having none of your own. And yet it was somehow more disturbing seeing them kneeling before you now, so synchronous in personality and appearance it is hard to tell them apart, with their battle-shorn heads and ears looped with gold and the self-assurance of gods. Their words were chosen to soothe, to charm, to coerce. It belied a ferocious sense of competition they had learned to navigate with silver tongues.

"We don't have time to leave the city. We must discuss what moves are to be made. Agapeto is talking of trade with the Lumms, but we think there is a better price to be found to the north. Trade, Mother. Finally a free market to move our goods without the King's taxes." Buccio says.

"Increase export, decrease import. Force the northern cities to buy our goods, all the while we become self-sufficient. It's possible now we can start to grow crops on royal land," Arabella says. "Imagine, Mother. Factories by the docks, jobs for a free Vardanel."

And so it begins, you think. The jockeying for power, the redivision of wealth. Exploitation is sure to follow. You let silence fall between you.

"Tell me how it was done," you say. "On the battlefield. Don't look at me like that, Buccio. Indulge me. Your talks of economics can wait."

You ignore their sighs, as they pull cushions to the floor and sit by your feet. Arabella proceeds to give an account of the final battle. Menas Glas and his men outnumbered them, but the army of the free Vardenel used the topography to their advantage, stationing archers in declivities the royal soldiers would not be aware of. She gives a blow-by-blow account, right up to the moment where she found you, screaming with triumph by the decapitated body. Everything she says rings true, but it is not how you remember it. How, in the darkest part of the night you thrust Wetgullet deep into the guts of Alwyn Glas, the crunch as you cracked open his innards. The cry of the king over the death of his only son. The look of surrender in his eyes as he realized you had bested him. It was intoxicating. To bring the most powerful man in the city to his knees. And then, he was dead. Arabella remembers you screaming in triumph, but it felt to you more like grief.

Buccio and Arabella begin to argue about whether Octavia or Felix had been the better marksman that night, but you feel absent from the conversation and their voices wash over you, until finally you say,

"Bring the corpse wax to me by evening, children. Then we will discuss the future."

* * *

You open gluey eyes to blue twilight. Outside, the distant sounds of a market vendor loading a carriage with his wares. How long did you sleep? It feels like minutes since the children left. Once again, you find yourself in the unnerving stillness of an empty house. Something feels amiss, an absence you can't shake. The head of Menas Glas has gone. Arabella and Buccio must have taken it, to protect you from yourself. Or there are darker forces at play here. There may be some royal sympathy still amongst the Owds, they could pool their powers against you. To convince you of your madness. Or worst still, reanimation. You should have told the children to burn the corpse. Even the most powerful Owds could not have brought back a king without a body.

Outside your chamber you find a small clay pot. Inside, a greyish goop, the corpse wax you had asked for. Maybe Arabella and Buccio saw this as a fitting exchange. The wax for the head. They had barely spent a minute inside the house since your return to the city. Did they spend their time plotting how they would kill you to gain legitimacy? The old days of imperial tradition may be on the wane, but the people still demanded blood to anoint. You would hand them power gladly, you had told them as much. What a way to die, destroyed by your own increase. If only Menas Glas were here, he would know a thing or two about parricide.

You retreat into your chamber with the corpse wax and take the box of matches by the paraffin lamp. You strike one and light the wax. The flame burns brightly and then extinguishes just as quick, followed by a terrible cloud of brown, billowing smoke. The smell is wretched. Dense, acrid fumes fill the air around you. Through the haze you see something worse yet to come. Smoke will fill the city within the year, huge industrial chimneys belching out noxious gasses into the air. Pollutants will drip into the mouth of the River Scorr. And tiny hands, mangled and bloodied, will be trapped in the teeth of great metal cogs. The people are screaming. Bones will burst out from their sallow skin, their skeletons crack as they reform into gargantuan machines. There will be a lifetime of labor for the citizens of Vardanel. You sacrificed everything for this. Your youth, the safety of your children (who you saw fit to bring into battle with you). Iones, Mateo, their deaths meant nothing. The fog clears and from the mist emerges the newly christened Victory Hill. Atop will stand Buccio and Arabella, locked in a sickening embrace, arms linked, as they push into each other until they will become one. A monster of your own creation.

The darkness comes quickly and you are grateful. The void is welcome after you see what is to come.

* * *

The bells rouse you, four notes chiming in an endless downward spiral. The smell of death permeates the room, the clay pot discarded on the floor, blackened by flame. As you rise stiffly from the old bed, a vertiginous feeling comes on and you hold onto the bedframe to anchor yourself. In the distance, you hear trumpets and, nausea rising, you realize they herald the victory parade. Those fools and their pageantry.

You run out onto Copeland Street, grey tresses billowing wildly across your face in the spring breeze. A convivial spirit runs throughout the city. The air is thick and heavy with wine and sweat, even though the hour is not past noon. Young girls are dressed in taffeta and sequins, their parents clasping tiny hands as they weave in and out of the drunks who sway across the street like streamers in the wind. A group of men are singing an old dockworkers song, lyrics changed to suit the occasion: *Fuck the King, He's dead, He's lost his fucking head.* Over and over again. Two women approach you on bended knee, tears glistening in their eyes. They thank you for freeing them. For bringing peace. You thank them, and ask them kindly for a cloak, and the younger woman hands hers over freely. You pull the hood up and make your way with the current of revelers to the market square. A stage has been erected and two people, dressed in crude likeness, enact the moment when you slew Menas Glas. A mighty roar goes up from the crowd and your heart pounds. The beating of a drum thuds through the people; they are compelled by a primal rhythm. The actors clear the stage and then there is Arabella and Buccio. They are dressed in swathes of mauve silk, your house colors. They look regal, triumphant. And in that moment, you realize that fate has already cast its die. Agapeto brings an engraved box onto the stage. The crowd bay, hungry to revel in your victory.

Buccio lifts the lid and, along with Arabella, they pull a head out of the box by the hair. But it is not Menas Glas.

The head is your own.

What They Don't Tell You About Training to Slay

By Katherine Quevedo

is that each callus roughens the easiest parts of you

(the hardest parts refuse to rough)

is that every cramp relaxes back open, yes, but the squeeze

dwells within you beyond where you can massage it out

(the tongue and heart are both muscles)

is that the enemy's eyes do not resemble

those of your trainer in the least

(they lack secret encouragement, and they destabilize

with how much they resemble your own)

is that dents on the surface do not equate to greater sharpness

—unless you let them

(and in that case, you may well throw out your training

and choose mercy)

The Marchers in the Fog

By Dariel R. A. Quiogue

"Edrique! Edrique!"

I turned to see the German, Strosser, shambling out of the fog, a dim shadow waving his arms over his head. I waved my harquebus over my own head, the better for him to see me. The fog was indeed that thick, and if you had asked me to shoot the side of a standing horse twelve feet away, por Dios, I do believe I would've missed. Our miserable little fire was dying, so it was no aid to finding me either. In time the German did see me, though, and he shuffled over.

"Have you seen my dog?" he rumbled.

I gestured at the sadly steaming black pot. "There."

Strosser blasphemed in his thick Bavarian dialect. Then he opened the lid, sniffed, and said, "Damme, Edrique, I wish you'd asked before you cooked her. She'd the makings of a good bird dog."

"It was as good a dog as a dog can be," I said, and Alvarez, slumped against a tree somewhere behind me, tittered. "We're hungry now. Better the dog, than chancing you missing a bird anyway in this fog."

The German grunted irritably and began to eat. I could see his big throat muscles work, protesting every lukewarm lump he forced down it. I could sympathize; I am a Castilian, born of a good family, a caballero family, and once I would have assured you it would be a cold day in Hell before my pride let me taste the flesh of horse, let alone dog. We've been in the coldest of Hells for months. Hell, I found, is a city somewhere in the Low Countries, a place only God remembers the name of now, for I would rather not.

We'd been sitting below her walls since spring. It was now nearing June, as far as I could reckon, but my sense of time was grown most unreliable. We only knew it was no longer winter because there was no more snow, but por Dios, if we had seen the sun a dozen times since the siege began, I'm the King of El Dorado. The entirety of Europe, it seemed, had been swallowed by a gray fog, colder than a witch's tits and damp as a toad's touch. The weather had been so foul there'd been no harvest in the country to speak of; even those villages we hadn't touched last year so they might grow food we could—as the military manuals say—requisition later, had nothing.

This I offer with complete certainty, because I had personally taken all those miserable peasants owned, at swordpoint, many times. That was our job, we cavalrymen—more than reconnoitering, more than hunting down our counterparts serving the House of Orange, we were expected to find food. That was before we ate our horses. Now, horseless, our new function was to picket the outer perimeter of the siege lines and, should the enemy come, to make as much noise dying as we could so the rest of the army might live. It was a cold, an enervating, and most of all, a *hungry* job.

Hunger and misery, exacerbated by the absence of the sun, do strange things to a man's mind. They start a spiral of decay, like the stairs in an old noble family's mansion, that lead first to the musty wine-cellar, then down to the dank depths of some hidden oubliette where unmentionable secrets lie. Madre de Dios, I think if that sly devil the Prince of Nassau himself had ridden down the road and offered me a basket of bread to leave this post, I'd have taken it. And that was by no means the worst act I contemplated.

Suddenly there was a crash and Alvarez swore, jerking my attention back to the fire.

Strosser had thrown the pot and its accursed contents into the embers, and now he and Alvarez were at each other's throats. More men from the troop were rushing up to join the fight.

"Bavarian dog!" Alvarez roared. "That was all our food for the day!" Strosser bellowed back something about "being man enough to go look for something better," but I don't remember exactly what he said, save that his Spanish was—as always—far from grammatical. But whatever he said, it was intelligible enough to Alvarez, who whipped out his long knife.

Two dark Andalusians, the Fanez brothers, pounced on the German and pinned his arms, yelling at Alvarez to strike. This I could not allow.

"Enough!" I cried, drawing my sword and interposing it between Alvarez and the German.

The sight of a sword, an officer's sword, stopped them—but only just.

"Let me gut the pig," Alvarez snarled. "By God, I'm so hungry I could eat German pig. Let me kill him!"

"Stand down, damn you!" I growled. "You want food? Then you'll join me in a scout around the perimeter. We'll check the villages along the way."

Alvarez' lip curled in contempt. "As if we hadn't done that a dozen times already in the last weeks. The Dutch have no more food than we."

"Peasants excel at hiding food," I retorted. "You may unleash your temper on them. Perhaps that's what we need to unlock their tongues, and their cupboards."

"Is that an order, Lieutenant?"

"Of course."

Alvarez straightened, sheathing his knife. "Then I obey. If the stinking farmers won't yield their stores, we'll have them instead. Or their wives. Or their children." His eyes were alight with the flame of incipient madness, and my intended rebuke for the monstrous thought died in my throat.

Instead I turned to Strosser, who at my nod was quickly freed by the Andalusians. "You will come with us," I told him, at which he uttered a surly grunt. He would be my counter to Alvarez, should the mercurial Andalusian snap completely.

"We've pillaged all the villages on the outer perimeter many times over, as Alvarez says. But the villages nearest the citadel are barely touched, on the General's orders. I say we go nearer the town this time, for better pickings. We can always say we got lost in the fog."

Alvarez surprised me by now agreeing with the German. "What he says is good, Edrique. We should get a taste of what the General's staff are keeping for themselves."

I nodded. And so our fates were sealed.

* * *

The fog—more like earthborne clouds by this point—billowed around us as we marched.

We could not keep any match alight at all, so between the twelve of us we had only my two wheellock pistols, one of which had misfired on me several times already. This one I thrust through the front of my belt, intending it to be the first shot; for if I had reason to fire twice, it were far better that the second shot be the surer. We walked with our swords loosened in our scabbards; Alvarez and Strosser carried their calivers, unloaded and unprimed, for intimidation. It was all woefully inadequate. We should have run when we came upon the village. We should have burned it all down. But we were fools.

It was Correa, who'd been a poacher before he enlisted, who first sensed the wrongness in the village. He stopped, cocked his head, then hissed, "It's too silent." He sniffed. "And there're no fires. Like nobody's been here for days."

"Search the houses," I ordered.

We fanned out, gray ghosts stalking through a grayer fog. The first house I entered was empty of life, its door yawning open. I stepped upon a child's biscuit doll, and its broken head lolled free, the glass eyes staring up at me. I cursed and crushed it under my boot heel. Only after I'd checked the pantry did I begin to realize something was badly amiss. There was a loaf of black bread there, untouched by man, yet riddled by maggots. If the inhabitants had fled, why had they left a whole loaf of bread? And what child would leave her beloved doll?

The next several houses were the same: abandoned, apparently in great haste, but with no signs of violence. Then Alvarez grabbed my arm. "Hsst! Hear that, Lieutenant?"

"What is it?"

"Knocking! And voices! I can't make out what they're saying, but it's coming from that house over there," and he pointed at another dwelling looming out of the murk.

We hurried to the house, and found it shut, the doors and windows boarded up with multiple planks hastily nailed—no few had been hammered awry, evidence of the hurry in which the deed had been done. At this, the men gave back and crossed themselves, for we Spaniards only do this thing to contain that which we dread most: the plague. I looked for the white skull mark and cross that was the universal sign painted on a plague house, but there was none.

Yet, the knocking and cries grew louder. "Please! Who's there? Let us out!"

The cries wrenched at my heart, for there were children's voices among them, but I steeled myself to give the only possible reply. "There is nothing we can do for those with the plague. I can only advise you to make your peace with God," I called back.

"It's not plague! For the love of God, please believe us—we have no plague! We're all hale! Please! We've been trapped in here for days!"

"What surety can you give me that there is indeed no plague here? And why else would you have been boarded up?" I called.

But it was Correa, the poacher, who gave me my answer. "Look, rats," he said in his laconic manner, jerking his chin at a pile of moldy hay. I saw a naked tail disappearing into the stack. "You never see rats in a plague town. They die of it first."

Then the voices started again. "Are you soldiers? You must be Spanish, from your accent. We're Catholics too! Let us out! We have food! Our liberty for food!"

I hesitated, for at the back of my mind was the thought that the inmates had yet to explain why they'd been boarded up in their own house. Perhaps I was to assume that, being Catholic, they'd been treated thus by their Calvinist neighbors. Still, I was not comfortable with the idea of letting them out without more questions. But Alvarez and Strosser, once again in surprising accord, had already started to prise away the boards, using their calivers as crowbars. I signaled the other men to pitch in, and within minutes they had the door open.

As soon as the last bar was off, the door flew open—and suddenly hands were reaching out and dragging my men in. Strosser bellowed in German, fear and pain loud in his voice, then there was a sickening crunch as his own sword, wrested from his hands, bit into his skull. The boarded house's inmates boiled out, tearing into my cavalrymen with grim, mad intent. They were ill-armed—a few kitchen knives, cudgels, rakes, hay forks and other farm tools—but they owned the strength of the possessed.

I discharged my first pistol, but the lock only spun and spat a sulfurous smell. Then they were upon me, and a farmwife with a maniacal expression was swinging at me with a scythe. I felled her with a sword stroke, the gorge rising in my throat. Beside me, Correa was fighting with sword and dagger drawn, and he dispatched another farmer. A child stabbed him with a kitchen knife, but was not strong enough to push the steel past his jack. I shot the child with my second pistol, my mind numb with the horror of the deed.

It probably took longer to tell it, but the vicious fight was soon over. Five of my men were dead, Strosser among them, but we had killed nine—men, women, a stripling boy, three children. Alvarez plunged into the house, his blood up with the transport of fear and exultation that comes with deadly combat—then he staggered back out.

"I know why they were boarded up," he croaked. "Madre de Dios, I wish I didn't. I wish I hadn't looked!"

"What did you find?" I said.

"Bones. Human. In the soup pot. And in the kitchen, an opened coffin. Dios mio, Dios mio, they were all boarded up for ghouldom!"

It was the answer I had dreaded. Perhaps I had known all along. "Let us be gone from here," I said.

But Alvarez wasn't finished. "Do you know," he choked out, shaking, "Do you know what was worst about it? I'll tell you. The smell of the soup—it made my mouth water." He looked back. "It made my mouth water."

"Out," I managed to croak, my heart too sick and my mind too shaken with unspeakable thoughts for more eloquence. I waved my men away with my sword, and warily, fearfully, they backed away from the charnel scene. Insane thoughts filled my head, and I could see from their faces the same was happening to them.

For a vagary of treacherous wind, so still for days, had drawn tendrils of scent from within the house. I had smelled the soup, and like Alvarez, it had made my mouth water. We left that village, truly desolate now, at a shambling, stumbling run.

* * *

Back in the false safety of our camp, the memory of that damned village continued to haunt us.

We were still hungry. We cut up strips of rawhide and boiled them into a miserable, bitter soup, its only saving graces its heat and the ghostly memory of the flavor of meat. Thereafter, two days passed with not even a biscuit to quiet our bellies and their murmurings. On the third morning, a courier on his way toward the siege camp made the mistake of passing by our fire. We relieved him of two stale black loaves and a fist-sized lump of bacon for his trouble. Shared between my nine remaining men and myself, though, they were but a drop in the proverbial bucket. If anything, that taste of pork only whetted our hunger more.

Once again, it was Alvarez who first gave voice to the unspeakable thought haunting all our heads. "That courier will have to ride past us again on his way back," he said, hollow eyes gleaming with ominous speculation.

"His horse," smiled one of the Fanez brothers in agreement.

"If we, His Majesty's own cavalry, have to walk, so can that blasted messenger," chimed in the other Fanez.

"Extorting food is one thing," I cautioned the men. "But taking an army courier's horse can be considered an obstruction of duty. In the General's eyes, that'll be treason." I think I still half-believed that when I said it. But only half, and my men, knowing me as well as I knew them, could sense the weakness I felt in my own argument.

"We're not obstructing his duty if we let him walk away, Lieutenant," said Alvarez. "Which we will. He just has to give up his horse."

"You rank him, sir," coaxed the elder Fanez. "Just say you're requisitioning it, officer's privilege. You could even give him a scrip to take to the Quartermaster-General for it." The men sniggered. The Quartermaster-General was known to be even more elusive to our prayers than God himself.

I stood up then from the saddle blanket on which I'd been sitting and made a show of putting on my hat. "Let me think about it while I stand a watch," I told them, thinking I had put the matter off decisively. They looked at each other. As I said, men get to know their officers as inevitably as officers get to know their men. And I was hungry, too.

* * *

In the gray murk that passed for dawn, we took our positions barring the road.

Anticipating that the courier would swing wide of our camp after yesterday's experience, then return to the road once safely past, we left a few men in the camp to tend a small fire, and stuffed brush and straw under our blankets to stand for our sleeping forms. Our ambush was laid well down the road, in a deceptively safe-looking spot—no brush, no trees, no houses. But the road on either side was flanked by irrigation ditches, their banks so steep even a rider would not perceive a man hiding in them until it was too late. We knew this well enough; it was where we'd lost some of our own horses, and a few good men too, to a Dutch ambush.

My plan was simple. Our prey was to be given no chance to resist. I had issued the Fanez brothers our last two lances, and hidden them on either side of the road. They were to spring out and stop the courier's horse, which at the time I was blinding myself to thinking of as our prey. The courier himself was supposed to be no more than an annoyance, so I stationed three more men about five yards from the Fanezes; they were to drag the courier off his horse and subdue him, with the flat of the blade if possible.

Alvarez and I took our stations a few yards farther down the road from the Fanezes, as the reserve. Again, we could keep no match alight. Thus, the only guns we had were my two wheellocks. Alvarez being our best pistol shot, I gave him the more reliable of the two pistols, tucking the other into my belt with the butt angled for a left-hand draw.

It was past mid-morning, almost noon, when we heard the clatter of hoofs.

"Here comes lunch," Alvarez hissed.

It is said that there are no memories clearer than those one wishes he never had. I can attest to the truth of it. I still see, still hear, still smell every last detail of the day I sealed my fall from grace in Flanders. The gray damp of the ever-present fog. The squelch and slither of boots in mud, and the stinks they released. The weight of my riding sword in my hand. The growing realization of the enormity I had committed myself to.

I had thought to let the courier live. Now I knew I'd been fooling myself all along—we were here not to extort a horse, but for murder.

We had not been unexpected. The courier came through our ambuscade warily, at a trot that could easily be turned into a gallop, a flintlock pistol in his hand.

The first Fanez to spring out was shot through the heart even as he cried out for the courier to stop. The other brother howled in rage, and ran in with the lance leveled as a pike. This the courier dodged, deftly dancing his horse away, even as he dropped the empty gun to draw his second pistol. My three swordsmen reached him then, only for the courier to blow one's brains away.

Alvarez and I fired our wheellocks at the same time. But the courier, desperate for his life, kept his horse dancing this way and that, so that when our guns went off with their customary delay—the wheellock's curse—neither man nor horse were where we'd aimed. We threw away the pistols and went in with cold steel.

The remaining Fanez was still trying to hold back the horse with his lance, while my other two swordsmen hacked futilely at both horse and rider. The courier was a good fighter, as couriers who must ride through enemy lines have to be, and while he was mounted he had all the advantages. Then Alvarez tried to seize the reins. The courier cried out in wrathful Asturian, hacking Alvarez' fingers off, forcing him to fall back, then wheeled the horse to ride me down. I was the last man standing in his path.

A black anger possessed me then. Who was this bastard to kill so readily two of my men? Who was he to deny us our need? The courier charged me in the French style, sword extended stiff-armed as a lance. I stood my ground, then dodged aside at the last minute, and as they passed I wrapped my left arm around the courier's waist while hammering my sword's pommel into his gut.

We both rolled into the mud. "The horse!" the surviving Fanez cried out in dismay. Receding hoofbeats punctuated our loss.

But the Asturian courier and I were already locked into our own world. He kicked me off. We both rolled to our feet with practiced speed, and then he was measuring his blade against my broad riding sword. My opponent was a good swordsman, but I was wild with fury, and with the fear that he too might get away and doom us all to the noose, and I had the heavier blade. Savagely, I beat at his guard until it crumbled and his sword fell from fingers hammered numb. Then, before he could draw his poniard, I dropped him to the earth with a heavy blow of the hilt.

The courier lay there gasping, all the wind knocked out of him. He wiped blood from his mouth and spat weakly at me. "Senor," he said thickly, "I know not your quarrel with me, but know that in attacking me you have not only invited yourself to the King's gallows but also proven yourself the basest of all men, ambushing a fellow-Spaniard and soldier for mere gold."

Alvarez, behind me, gave a strangled giggle. "Did we ask you for your coin the first time? No, we wanted to roast your horse!"

Suddenly the Asturian smiled, the smile of a brave man who knows the inevitability of his fate. "I have thwarted you, then," he said. "For instead of my noble steed, you only have me."

A tremor went through me then. I had been drawn—I had let myself be drawn—across a line, with my soul and salvation left behind on the other side. "Yes, we have you," I said to the Asturian, then plunged my sword through his heart.

As my men bent to the necessary work, we became aware of a large column approaching through the fog. The shapes slowly resolved into peasants, several score of them, all armed, all in rags, all of them with a mad light in their eyes. Wordlessly, they flowed around us and folded us into their number. Wordlessly, they plunged into the task of preparing our meat, and wordlessly we shared it.

I should've been stronger. I should've argued for what I knew was right. I should've run away. But I did none of those things. Instead I ate. I sated myself, and wanted more. I left my humanity behind in that all-covering, soul-leaching fog.

We marched through the gray countryside, and when we met bands of Spanish and Flemish soldiers also pillaging, we hallooed them and invited them to partake of our bounty. Through the gray mists we marched, in dozens at first, then scores, then hundreds. History will blench and forget our names, as is proper. We ceased, most of us, to care. We marched, and all who would not join us went down beneath our knives and into our pots. We were the marchers in the fog, and we left nothing living in our wake. I learned to distinguish the subtle nuances of flavor between Dutchman and Spaniard, German and Walloon.

When at last the fog lifted, we were no longer an army, but a locust-like horde. The horrified General threw his own cavalry at us, and when we fled to a marsh, he blanketed the entire place with cannon fire. I crawled away, wounded in body but worse in the mind. History records the event as a military debacle, a tale of mutineers changing flags and being wiped out for their perfidy. Now you know differently—but you will keep the secret to yourself.

Eventually I made my way back to Spain, and though my wounds had healed, I could not bring myself to rejoin the army. I live under an assumed name, in a remote mountain village where no one knows my face.

And there are days, when the fog rolls in, that the unholy craving comes upon me again, and I go out with my sword and gun. Into the fog, to look for lonely travelers. Strangers. Like you.

The Festering Mantle

By J.M. Hayes

Like a winter gale, braying voices hurtled towards the eyot of Rusholme. Upon the eyot, Lord Maugrith and his companions, with hammering hearts, clasped their sword-hilts and spear-shafts, now met with their fateful hour. Their dread-weapons poised, glinting in the dusk, the clamor crashing upon them on all sides. Hoving into view, however, caught in the fading rays of daylight, the last southering geese passed over the island, honking and shrieking as they went. At their passing, the weapons sagged in their grips, and Maugrith and his comrades settled down once again, hidden amidst the lanky rushes. A cold air blew through Maugrith's body, a balm of hollow comfort.

Few knew of Rusholme, low and green, a verdant wen on the waters of Órbrithion, which was clept also Misshaft. For league upon league stretched the perilous marshes of Misshaft, with only a few ancient trackways passing over the noisome, bottomless mires. Many islands like low hills broke the marsh's surface;

dry-earthed and distant, they stood fortress-like in the mighty fens. Carrs rose here and there also where the land was firmest; such a one soared near Rusholme, its willows and alders rising as palisades against the dawn, shielding the island's view of the east.

Though the marsh's waterways were bereft of men—its horizons scarce even of farmsteads—it was unwise for one to light fires during the day, for the smoke might carry and betray one to watchful eyes. For this reason, Maugrith and his companions—Welland, Arundel, and Eryl—waited till the last glimmer of day vanished before lighting a fire in the shallow pit. The frosty wind ever seemed to rise as Elfring set, greeting all with the night's icy kiss, and the men pulled at their woollen cloaks, binding their arms tight across their chests, shivering, bracing themselves for the fireless hour of twilight.

Amid the frozen gloom, Lord Maugrith's mind turned towards Ramfrey-King Alwyn, their secret guest in the island's rush-built hide. Gazing upon the hovel, sunk into the side of the eyot, Maugrith heard no sound coming from it, save for the evening breeze groaning through the gaps of the driftwood door.

Lord Welland, with his hand fixed fast to his sword-hilt, raised his head and surveyed the company. Eyeing the sharp glint of his blade, Welland broke the quietude and asked aloud, "So what says our liege? Has he spoken today?"

Eryl the swain—charged with providing the king's meal—shook his head.

"No, my lord," said Eryl, trembling in the evening chill. "Save for 'Thank you' and 'Peace be with you.'"

Welland, dropping his gaze to his half-sheathed sword, muttered to himself, "And so the ordinance remains." Maugrith said nothing, but looked on in silence upon the hide. A curlew's call sprang up from the far reeds, catching Lord Maugrith's attention. Listening as its warbling cries melted into the air, ringing gloomily across the marsh, he was reminded of the first night upon Rusholme. He had said nought of what he saw that night. It pricked his thoughts like a needle, stinging him during all his hours, both waking and sleeping. In the weary glow of twilight, it was difficult for him to read the faces of his companions, to descry whether or not they too had seen what he had seen that night.

As far as Maugrith could recall, King Alwyn had spoken little since their landing upon Rusholme. The journey that led them there had been a hard one. Fearing to put their trust into strangers—even amongst their own folk—they sought for the island by canoe guideless, using only the sun by day and the stars by night as way-finders. Upon finding the safe haven of Rusholme, Maugrith and his companions drew plans for the days ahead: to make the eyot fit for a camp, to muster what loyal kinsmen they could from far and wide, and to strike back against the foe with ambushes and lightning raids. Then, on behalf of the whole company, Maugrith approached the king and presented him with their designs. But King Alwyn forbade them.

"Hold your peace, my friends," said Alwyn. "Stay you all upon this island. No man must sally forth or venture without my say. For now, look to the eel traps, collect firewood for the shallow pit, and ensure that a fresh loaf and a flask of boiled water is left for me each day. Leave me be for now and disturb me not. Have faith in our patroness, the Lady Wisdom, who has led us here; forsooth, we are in Her hands. Keep faith in Her, Maugrith, as you would in me."

Having thus spoken to Maugrith, Alwyn slipped away silently into the hide and locked fast the door. Maugrith liked not the commands, mistrustful as he was of the Lady Wisdom. He knew not what manner of thing she was: others though, Alwyn above all, lauded her as divine guardian of his kingship, protectress of the throne of the Ramfrey, which is to say, Ravenlord. But Maugrith thought otherwise. He himself knew neither her quality nor her purpose; she was but a mystery, an insufferable enigma that hid from all reason. Why should he place his trust in the wisdom of a ghost-wife, a daydream, and not in that of Alwyn, his lord the

Ramfrey, his friend of many winters? Lest his mind bend toward mistrust of Alwyn, Maugrith chose instead to regard the king the author of his own wisdom, granting nothing to the she-spirit. It was only he in whom Maugrith could place his trust. In this manner, Maugrith relayed the Ravenlord's commands to the company, who each faithfully fulfilled them. Once Elfring had set that night, a fire was lit and the men laid resting round about it. Sleep overtook them, save for Lord Maugrith, who had agreed to take the first night watch.

As the others slept in their wicker shelters, Maugrith sat close-by, gazing out towards the marsh's horizons. With not even the light of Eveshone to aid him, Maugrith's vision fell deeper and deeper into the surrounding darkness; his heart quickened as phantom enemies rose and sank amid the tangled blackness; wading spearmen vanished into dead trees; the splash of falling twigs faded into the pawfalls of war-hounds. Amid the stillness, dangers seemed to abound, lurking in the secreted realm of night. With a heavy breath Maugrith sighed; he closed his eyes and opened them as he steadied his heart.

"These dangers are merely tricks of the mind," reasoned Maugrith amid the shadows of night. "They will harm us not. The true peril I shall await, and be ready, if it may come."

No sooner had the thought passed when from out of the carr,

like a clap of thunder, there came a piercing shriek. Maugrith's blood rimed in his veins. Then soundlessly, entering into the dreadful stillness, a pale mass came gliding out from betwixt the adumbral trees. Maugrith beheld the mass soaring in long, shallow gyres over the fens, screaming across the marshy air. Its shriek was to him alike a woman's voice, mingled with fright and fury. All the wild and terrible shapes of Maugrith's imaginings returned and came alive to him in that moment, congealed in the likeness of that white bird, that corpse-fowl. He shuddered as he perceived its pallid wings, its unseen, beshadowed face. He knew not what it was: some night demon? A witch? Or yet, perhaps, Lady Wisdom herself, come finally in her true form? Without a single flutter, the hellion drew closer to the king's hide, its screams becoming louder and more piercing; then, as quick as thought, it dived and disappeared, swooping into the hide. At once Maugrith sprang up and stood unmoving, listening and watching intently; neither sound nor movement emerged from the hide. All thought of the watch and his companions left him. As the hours of night passed, Maugrith waited still, impatient for any trace of the king's safekeeping. Dawnlight and its bright chorus crept up on Rusholme. With each breaking golden ray, Maugrith sank to the ground. Soon afterwards, Eryl arose and kindled the oven. Removing a new loaf from the mud-built stove, Eryl strode over to the hide and left it by the king's door. Maugrith watched on as a hand emerged from the open door, took up the meal and pulled the door shut.

Even after these many days, Maugrith would not speak of that night's visitation, deeming the matter better left unsaid. By this, so reasoned Maugrith, the company's fragile peace may yet be preserved. As the last rays of Elfring darkened, the flame pit was lit, and the cold winds abated.

* * *

Maugrith awoke with a start as Lord Arundel shook him.

"Maugrith, awake," Arundel whispered. "I have fulfilled my watch. I shall leave you to yours."

Weary, Maugrith eased himself off the ground and staggered towards the fire pit. Sitting with his back to the flames, he refreshed himself with a flask of boiled water and waited as his eyes grew used to the gloom. The flame behind him crackled and echoed across the brackish waters; the world beyond was hushed, lying drear beneath the moonless sky, hoping for Elfring's return. As Maugrith awaited the coming of the dreaded vigil hours, a strange savor intruded upon him. It was almost imperceptible at first, but slowly, with thieving pace, the scent grew, and grew, growing more steadily into clarity. As he sniffed the still air, the odor seemed to him dull yet fetid, mortal, as lifeless as the stench of battle. It was the smell of things falling apart, time melting away. For all its dullness, the putrid fume lingered, drifting in and about the island, blanketing it in a fog of miasma. Maugrith peered deep into the wall of shadow but saw nothing, at least naught that he should heed. Having gotten up, he wondered about the camp, looking for the cause of the odor. After a while, he traced the course of the stench's beginning, where it was most pungent: the king's hide.

Into his mind poured all the remembrance of the winged beast: gliding with still wings from the trees, shrieking with the fen's wrathful dirge. An icy dread crawled through his flesh, his mind's eye awash with terrible imaginings. Growing fearful for the king's sake, Maugrith crept towards the hide. Straining to hear for any noise, he could perceive only soft murmurings wafting from within. Pressing his ear to the hide's door, he could not tell what was being spoken, but only that it had the likeness of a conversation held in a low voice. The more he listened, the more he thought he could hear the sound of one voice speaking alone.

Amid the heightened hush, Maugrith knocked upon the door. The murmuring ceased.

"My king, my king," Maugrith with foreboding hissed. "May I enter?"

A reply came swiftly from within.

"Leave me be," said the voice softly. "Do not fear; all will be well. Peace be with you."

Then there was silence for a while, but soon the sound of veiled whispering renewed within. Returning to the fire, Maugrith steadily seated himself down, taking up again his vigil in disquietude. Dry were his lips, restless his mind, like unto the flicker of firelight. Calm and strangely serene seemed the voice to Maugrith; an almost womanly touch to it, he thought. The very notion of it haunted him, chilling him with a sepulchral coolth even as the dawn's warmth approached. Not long afterwards Eryl awoke to kindle the oven. With the oven lit, he approached Lord Maugrith with hushed steps and, with due reverence, hailed him. Not a word passed Maugrith's lips, but he sat staring into the carr beyond, his face behued with the pallor of dread.

Eryl, thinking some concern gripped his lord's attention, stared also into the eastward carr. The trees stood stark against the voluminous clouds, aflame in the dawn's light; golden orange, like evening bonfire smoke, they shone bright between the trees, even before Elfring's rising.

Bending to meet Maugrith, in gentle tone he asked his lordship, "Pardon, my lord: what is it that you see?"

After a moment of quietness, Maugrith's eyes lifted and studied the brightening clouds. Then, rolling down, they fixed their gaze again upon the carr.

"I see fire," came Lord Maugrith's voice, as still as the morning air. "I see the Hall of Ardor burning, the mighty Royal Gates blazing, the shadow of our foes' spears into the courtyard marching. I behold the purple mantle festering upon kingly shoulders, its smell stinking the air—and our patron goddess, radiant as a star, gazing upon our fallen kinsmen, laughing."

Steadily the morning tide of birdsong rose from the carrs and greeted the silent watchers. Leaving Maugrith seated upon the earth, Eryl returned to the oven, a shadow upon his face.

* * *

Beneath the bright winter sun, the breeze gathered apace, shaking the reeds into whisper. Maugrith went about his work pulling in the eel traps—mud-caked, reeking of the marsh—heaving them from the bank of the eyot. Under the face of the fen, below its sun-glowing rushes, he could see the peril unmasked in the daylight. Before his eyes was the door of the hide and the voice from within. Not a moment passed when those memories did not arise, compassing all that he saw. The bonds of the traps slumped weakly in his grip, his gaze falling away into darkest thought.

Later, as dusk approached, Lord Arundel came and assisted Maugrith with the traps. As the last eel was dropped into the hemp-sack, Arundel turned looking upon Maugrith.

"My swain has been gravely quiet today," said Arundel, as he tied a knot in the sack's neck. "I could see his hands trembling whilst making bread. You know me best, Maugrith, I am not a man who takes lightly the tremoring of men's hearts, so I took him aside and had him apprise me of the cause of his fears. He informed me of all that you had told him this morning. It seems plain to me that he is greatly concerned for you and by truth, my friend, I cannot forswear that I have my worries also."

Maugrith kept his silence, squatting as he watched the eel trap fall back into the grim waters. Planting a firm hand on Maugrith's shoulder, Arundel crouched down, bringing his lips closer to his ear.

"Do you know what Lord Welland presently busies himself with?" Arundel whispered. "He strides about the camp, his eyes fixed upon the floor, muttering to himself I know not what. I have seen his hand flutter about his sword-hilt, loosening and tightening at every moment. Doubtlessly he grows weary with patience and, day by day, that weariness strengthens; he might even go forth from the island, against our liege's command. If he leaves, the bond of trust will surely be broken. How long will our king fare here, amid Misshaft, if we are not one? The trust must remain whole—it cannot fail. But I cannot entrust Eryl alone to help me keep the company here on Rusholme." The grip of Arundel's hand tightened on his shoulder. "I must have you by my side; I cannot have you lost among the sorrows of yesteryear. I must have you strong—as like of old—a steady hand by my side, should all else fail. Do you understand, Maugrith? Soon enough, by our king's word, we shall have our vengeance; but for now, will you not take my hand and share with me all our burdens?"

Like a gift between noble friends, Arundel offered to Maugrith his open hand. Staring down upon it, he held the hand wearily in his gaze. Lifting his eyes to meet Arundel's, Maugrith smiled and clasped fast his lordly companion's hand in his. Such a token of trust Maugrith could not refuse, and how eagerly did he receive it. Arundel's hand felt sun-warm, and his eyes shone with noontide luster, casting away the heaviness of fear and doubt. And yet, even as the smiles of the two lords met, there loomed before Maugrith a shape. Gliding from the rays of light, it had the likeness of pale wings. The grin upon his face fell away, his heart shivering, his mind eclipsed by the shadow of the winged beast, by the fumes of the festering stench. Arundel furrowed his brow, beholding the darkness in Maugrith's eyes.

Daylight dimmed as clouds mustered in the evening sky, sped on by freezing winds. Beholding the brightness of Arundel's eyes, the fear within Maugrith allayed and relinquished its hold upon his senses. His hands still clasping Arundel's, Maugrith felt, at last, the pangs of urgency, the desperate desire to speak of those things left unsaid. Leaning in towards his companion, Maugrith murmured:

"On the first night, here on this island, I saw something... it came from the forest. It glided from out of the trees; its wings were white and motionless; it screamed a woman's scream. Then, after a while, it swooped from the air and entered the Ramfrey's hide. From that night onwards, I have not seen it leave the king's abode; no sign of him have I espied, but the smell, that stench: can you not smell it? It comes from that very place. I have besought our liege, I asked for his reply... and he did not give answer—but someone else did. It was a voice, a lady's voice, soft and serene. I am afraid, Arundel... I fear for the king's safety. That damned mistress, Lady Wisdom, the pale thing, whatever it is, holds him prisoner—I am sure of it!"

Releasing his grip, Arundel turned away from Maugrith.

"Our king, enthralled to a demon—which you name as the very Lady Herself! You speak boldly, friend," said Arundel starkly. "And I would have dared said that you regaled me with wild tales, had it been a matter trifle in kind; yet you speak of our king's Blessed Patroness! Has not Alwyn ever given thanks to the Lady for all that he has received: his prosperity? His throne? His wisdom? Is not Her image upon our very broaches? Was it not you yourself who said that the king bids us trust Her, as we would him? Why now do you say otherwise? What has caused you to speak foul of her, to be so certain of Her ill intent?"

"Is it not clear enough, Arundel?" answered Maugrith, sharp as an arrow. "Has she not revealed before us and made naked her true self? What protectress would veil danger from our eyes? What mighty she-spirit would betray her servant and allow his kingdom to fall? Would we now be hiding like cowards in the fens, to await the day when Lord Swike and the Men of Drizenryke come upon us, if such a *thing* had been for our good? Ever have I distrusted her, knowing not why the king would impute his wisdom to phantoms. But my king have I trusted; for him I live, and not a single peril, not even Misshaft, will gainsay it. Yet for how long have we remained here? When last did we hear from him? Not since that night, when the thing flew into his abode. And now we have silence... and the smell of decay, a stench of kingship in fetters rotting."

Arundel glanced towards the hide. Though he was certain he could not smell that perfume of decay, Arundel had nought else to say to Maugrith's argument.

"Yes, we must stay together," Maugrith said. "But we must, before all else, protect Alwyn King. There is nothing more important! I would, with all my bones, break the ordinance that he had bidden me, if it would save him from her. You asked me for aid, Arundel, and I pledged it; will you not likewise pledge it to me?"

Straightening himself up, Arundel swung his gaze towards the camp, contemplating it. From afar a curlew called, filling the stillness between the two lords. Before leaving, Arundel beheld Maugrith again and answered him:

"The days are flying before us, Maugrith; they will not halt for our sake. We have become prisoners of our own making, pressed upon every side: Welland, impatient, longs for blood; and the king, we know not why, keeps swye. Something must change: whether now is the time I know not, but we must act, lest someone else acts in our idleness. But let us for now leave off these thoughts. Elfring is setting and soon it will be night. In the morning we shall gather with Welland and Eryl and go before the king. Until then, keep courage, my brother, and remember my words. Safeguard the king, as well as I know that you will, as you tend to your watch."

With this, Arundel made his way up the bank, leaving Maugrith to the darkening rushes. As Arundel sat down for the hour of twilight, his thoughts were ever on Maugrith. Though troubled by the thought of what deeds Maugrith's fears would drive him to, Arundel assured himself, entrusting to his friendship—and the promises for the morrow—to assuage Maugrith's fevered impulses. And yet, notwithstanding his own assurances, the shadow of doubt lingered with him. More than ever, as the sun vanished beyond the west, Arundel dreaded the coming of night.

* * *

Lord Welland, having finished his watch, stirred Maugrith awake and retired to his wicker shelter. As with every night, Maugrith arose and took his seat close by the fire, keeping vigil as he surveyed the shrouded fen. As the marsh breathed its nocturnal sighs, the half-shapes of danger, cloaked amid the swarthy ripples and the scheming rushes, drifted into view. Watching as the fantasies of doom faded in and out of sight, like motes of dust caught in the sunlight, he wondered whether Arundel's promise was as phantasmal—and false—as they. The wind, rousing from its slumber, blew icily upon the vigilant lord, biting at his fingers; embracing himself, he ached for the dawn and its all-unveiling illumination. Closing his eyes, he could see, in the darkness of his mind, Arundel, Welland, and Eryl, half-lit and gathered without him. With bowed heads, they muttered among themselves; from under brows bedimmed by shadows, Arundel's voice, graver than the others, lifted to Maugrith's ears. "What shall be done with him?" said Arundel, his eyes suddenly darting towards him, glinting like tomb-candles in the grey light. "He is too weak. He cannot be trusted with the king's life. We must act with haste." Maugrith's sight drew towards the king's door as the dim light fell upon it, limp and ashen beneath its beams, lifeless but for the groan that sighed from within, like the wind in the grave.

Seeking release from the grim vision, Maugrith threw open his eyes. As steam into the winter air, the huddled shapes and the deathly groan vanished. All was quiet, save for the reeds rustling upon the eyot's margin, and the leafless boughs shaking in the forest. And then, from out of the night's silent depths, there came a voice calling to him. Above the wind's pitch he could hear it clearly; meek and gentle it sounded, as sweet as a lady's song beneath the rosy bower. No soul could he see, as though hidden deep in the evening's folds.

"O Maugrith," the voice uttered, hailing him. "Keep faith with your friends. Be strong for them, for your king's sake. Before you lies darkness, wherein there is no hope of forgiveness."

As he listened, the memory of that voice escaped him, lost in the murk of his beleaguered thoughts. Then, with sudden fleetness, as when an ember rushes spitting hot from the flames, the likeness of that voice came to Maugrith. A great shadow befell his heart, hearing in that very moment the voice that came from the hide.

"Ha! Is it you?" Maugrith rasped into the night. "Are you not she who spoke to me in the king's stead? You that have burdened my soul with dreams of despair! What manner of hateful thing are you?"

"I am such that tends to the king's good," came the response full of majesty. "I strive for no other purpose. Calm yourself, Maugrith, and leave the king to my care; if you do not have faith, and quell your rash desires, you will be the death of—"

"Silence!" snapped Maugrith with rage upon his lips. "I shall hear no more of it. You dare upbraid me, worthless sprite—tormenter—hell-queen! You speak with such gall! What right have you to imprison my king? I shall not hesitate to slay you, witch. Damn you, release him!"

Swiftly the voice died away, engulfed by the clamor newly risen from the eastern carr. As blood thundered in his ears, Maugrith descried the roaring of many voices, the clashing of spears upon iron-clad shields, the snarling of hounds. Gazing into the darkling woods, he saw—faint at first, now swelling—row upon row of torches blazing, their crimson tongues leaping, licking the air and seizing all things in their terrible glare. Then, like a frothing wave crashing upon the shingle shore, the festering stench arose, filling Maugrith's nostrils with its sickness. As the flashing night wheeled about him, he saw still before him the king's hide, glowing with the radiance of the fiendish torches.

Bounding towards the hide, Maugrith rained his fists upon the door. Nothing but the roaring of the host of Drizenryke could he hear.

"My king! My king!" bellowed Maugrith. "Open the door. Open, please!"

More clearly could he perceive the hateful cries of the enemy swamping the island. A thought dazzled his mind: if the king does not now fly from Rusholme, the foe will surely seize him.

"Alwyn, will you not listen to me? We must flee; the enemy has us. O my king, I can smell your mantle rotting upon your shoulders! Damnable witch! Will you not release him from your spell? Oh, how I long to stick you with my blade. Open the door; I say, open it!"

As the lord heaved with all his strength against the door, it gave way, splintering before him. Like a sudden gust of wind, with sword unsheathed, Maugrith threw himself madly into the darkness of the hide. His blade bit into flesh.

As the dimness dissipated, the whites of the king's eyes shone, gazing back upon Maugrith's face. Blood gurgled from his lips, falling thickly upon his immaculate, purple cloak. Flashing in the half-light, like a shard of glass, the sword protruded from the king's breast. As his book and quill-pen fell from his grip, Alwyn's mortal frame slumped to the floor, breathing out his last. As quickly as it had come, the clamor faded, melting into the winter gale; the fiery brands snuffed out into the breaking dawn, burning scarlet between the trees; the odor of decay vanished, bequeathing nothing but the scent of the marsh lingering about the eyot. Maugrith collapsed upon his knees, beholding Alwyn unstirring. As the air groaned in the hide, the emptiness yawned within him, swallowing Maugrith whole. Not a word did he utter, powerless as it was before the regal corpse. Lying upon the floor, the fallen book revealed the last of Alwyn's wisdom, gleaming wet on the page; written in the royal tongue, it read:

Mírdani bero is lendha árdi hin namni nácelisich
('What help is a king to his people if he is not patient?')

Out of the corner of his eye, Maugrith saw a shape high above him, dark against the new-born light streaming through the eastward window. There, he beheld the figure of an owl perched upon the sill; cold-white were its feathers, though gilded were they about its crown and nape; its head was like a cowl falling down into cloak-like wings, folded tightly against its body. As the light grew brighter, Maugrith could plainly see, not the face of some night-faring fowl, but the countenance of a woman: fair and beautiful was she, with eyes sparkling blue like the sun-drenched sea. Lowering her head, the owl-wife dropped her gaze to Alwyn's form, paying no heed to the silent lord beside him. A tear streaked her pearly cheek, glimmering silver in the dawn. As her breast swelled, she sighed softly and, with outspread wings, alighted from the sill. Taking wing, she cried a long and mournful note as she went, her dulcet lament for Alwyn King. Washing across the face of the fens, her voice seemed sweeter than Maugrith had remembered it during the watch of dread. Then, into the roseal rays of morn she glided, vanishing from human sight.

As the night visitor departed, a great darkness from the doorway loomed over Maugrith. Turning aside, he saw his three companions stood frozen before him. Lifeless as stones, their visages were vacant and void of spirit, for they had found themselves come too late to King Alwyn's aid. In their sight, they could see only their king lying stolen by a blade, and, to his side, the form of a wretch, wild-eyed, kneeling silently in the dark. Not one word was shared between them, for their speech died upon their tongues.

As noon arrived, the lords, having removed the blade from his noble breast, bound the Ravenlord in his mantle, fastening it tightly about him with his broach. Lifting him, they carried

Alwyn down to the bank of the eyot, laid him in the canoe, and placed all his blessed riches—his sword, his quill, his book—upon him. With a gentle push, the canoe was launched into the flow of Misshaft's waters; soon the tide bore king and canoe away, taking them far from troubled lands and beyond—when day was spent—into the great and silver seas. The lips of the three lords were sealed, their gazes turned to the greying earth. Grasping the newly baked bread in his hand, Eryl stared at it as though it were a stranger in their midst. After an hour it seemed, the swain with a mighty gasp cast the loaf into the blazing oven. Catching alight, the bread burst into flames, consuming the walls of the oven. The smoke billowed thick and black, climbing higher than the towering alders; the wind blew against it, carrying it far yonder the marshland's border. Quietly the four men stood upon Rusholme, as motionless as the ruins of old, and waited. Day speeded into the west and still the men stood upon the island. Then, after hours of waiting, the sound of voices drifted in from the darkened east. Shouts and cries of hatred broke in upon the company, who beheld now the blaze of torches gathering in upon them. The air rang with the clanging of shields, and the savage yelp and growls of slavering war-hounds. As the west glowed crimson with the final rays of Elfring, the companions stood—their hands clutching their sword-hilts and spear-shafts, their hearts trembling no longer—now ready for the hour of fate.

Respite

By R.H. Berry

Come,

Sit by my fire—

Your exhaustion shows in the drag of your steps

Your thirst, in your cracking, smacking lips

Your hunger in the faded bloodstains on your teeth.

I've pelts to share.

I've meat to roast.

Let the snapping embers soothe

While you quell the ache in your gullet.

The night must be so cold,

And it's clear you've travelled long,

With limited success

When it comes to the hunt.

You look to be carrying little, poor thing,

Not enough to skin your prey

Let alone tempt it close.

I don't wish to presume,

But if I will not offend,

I have some advice.

If you're weary and starving,

Stop chasing the game.

With suitable bait, it will come to you.

Offer food,

Give it comfort,

And I guarantee

It will forget to fear

A stranger in the dark.

       Now hold still.

Towards a Justice

By Matt Holder

When I found the fallen knight he slumbered underneath a dead tree, his drooping back propped against the white bark. Behind him the land sloped upward and became the mountain, endless fire and black smoke belching from its blasted summit.

They did not know how long the knight had been there, the little ones told me, only that in their morning play they strayed beyond the safe bounds of our village and their eyes caught the glint of the man's burnished plate.

You can use this man, she told me. *With his help you can close the mountain, sew close the tear in our home.*

Her eyes argued stronger than her words, and I spent the remaining morning in meditation to prepare. Accompanied by the endless giggling of my children, I recalled the strange and secret language to my tongue and spoke aloud the words of our magics. In my hands I called the flame and held it to my chest before breathing it into my lungs.

I approached the knight with confidence, old hatreds flaring. Distant cracks from the thundering mountain rumbled through the earth and rattled my teeth.

He did not lift his head at my step, and for a moment I thought him perished.

"You are far from your home," I said. Closer, I noted how tarnished his plate had become, cracked all through, and underneath it, the mail shirt resembled only a collection of rust. A cracked shield rested across his legs, and a sword without its scabbard lay at his side, as if dropped without care. He bore no helm, so when he stirred at my words I saw his gaunt face rise to meet mine. Taut-stretched skin, thin hair hanging as white threads, cheeks that sucked into his skull: his visage echoed all of the knights I had seen after they abandoned their war. This one was missing an eye, though the other sank so far into its socket I thought the man completely blind.

"My home is gone," the man said, his eye rolling about and catching the light.

I knelt before him. "Spare me your melancholies. Your home is not gone, but your people have abandoned you. This is your home now," gesturing toward the bursting mountain behind him, "as it is mine. And you will help me heal it. There is a group of cultists at the top, and I am old; I cannot fend back a swarm, for all my remaining power. Your sword-arm will carve my way to the summit, where I will seal its rupture."

The knight's head lolled left and right as if on a pendulum, and for a moment I was convinced the man's wits had abandoned him. "Why would I help you, sorcerer? Maybe I came here to die under this tree. Maybe I am tired of fighting. Or maybe the thought of aiding an enemy is enough to make me sick," and here he tried to spit in my direction, but his lips only flapped, dry and split from the winds.

"I have water. Here, drink." He seized my canteen with greed and proceeded to guzzle. As he shifted forward, his wretched scent assaulted my nostrils; rot mixed with the familiar odor of unwashed flesh, and under it all the metallic tang of blood.

"You will help me because you have nothing better to do, warrior. Your people broke this land and lost your war. Those left behind, like yourself, wander, untethered and unmoored. I offer you an anchor, soldier, a purpose to endear yourself to something other than your kind's lust for power. With your help I can close off this portal, redeem this land, and make safe my people. You will have done good."

"I am done with sermons," he spat, this time fresh spittle dribbling from his lips. "I go where I please, and my sword-arm is not for hire. Thank you for the water, but leave me in peace."

He tossed the canteen and leaned back against the tree.

"I was not asking, you stupid man," and I stood and breathed out the flame. Invisible, it snaked through the air at my bidding until it rimmed the knight's armor. The edges began to glow a dull orange, slowly brightening. Smoke curled from the glimmering plate. Panic setting in, the knight scrambled to his feet, wincing as his skin started to scorch and blister, trapped inside a growing forge.

"Curse you and your devil magics," he seethed. He tried to step forward, hand on his sword, but the invisible flames grew, rooting him in pain. A scream, not like a warrior's shout but more a child's wailing, tore from his lungs.

"You will help me ascend the mountain," I said, holding the ground between us, locked onto the frenzied gaze of his good eye. "You will protect me from the cultists. If you do not, I will boil you alive in your own pitiful armor. Is that the death you seek, noble knight? To die like an animal, mewling before its better?"

Breathing in, I relented the flame. The armor grew dim, and, when the knight ceased his seizing, the broken man looked at me and caught me in his stare. Murder and hate blazed in his gaze, but I reflected back in kind.

"Let's go climb your mountain, sorcerer."

* * *

We followed the old paths, laboring up the barren slope. Since the mountaintop began to expel its evil flames, the lush green of the pathways and ridgeline had burned, replaced now with cracked stone and scorched earth. Ash grew thick as we ascended, and I passed the clanking knight a cloth to hold over his mouth.

"Why do you need my sword-arm, old man? You seem more than capable of handling a few cultists."

I withdrew my own mask and tied it around my mouth. "There is a difference between confronting a broken and solitary opponent and battling a dozen crazed zealots. I have made this journey before and been turned away by their tenacity. Were I in my prime I would call down the sun and incinerate their bones to dust. But my prime is gone."

"Is there no one in your village that could help?"

"There is no one in my village that I am willing to sacrifice on a fool's errand."

"A fool's errand," the knight said. He stopped and turned to me. Sweat sheeted down his skeletal face. "Can you not close this mountain? Stop the devils from coming?"

Before answering I looked at the sun, noting its position. Any further delays and we would encounter the cultists at nightfall, when they inhaled their poisons and unleashed their berserker strength upon each other, endlessly burning and peeling their flesh as offerings for their demon-gods.

"It is possible that the situation is not beyond repair. But this mountain has burned for years now. The wound is large and flows freely. When your leg is cut and you do not treat the flesh, but instead let the blood flow and the flies gather and the maggots grow, what hope is there for the limb?"

"Then you lead me to suicide? Do you pit my own vainglory against your own?"

I laughed, then, and clapped the man on the shoulder. Clouds of ash billowed from the contact. Beyond the knight, I saw the shores of the magma-black plateau, where the lava flow pooled and churned. The summit was close.

"Your vainglory cannot hope to match my own, sir knight. Make haste. The enemy nears."

* * *

Our plateau crossing was not without incident. The knight, clumsy in his armor, stumbled more than once, forcing my hand to save him from the lake of fire. Along the way the bones of past cultists marked the trail. Black eyes and smiling teeth, charred ribs, cracked spines—all given gladly, if the stories were to be believed. I have no need for belief, however, for I have seen with my own eyes the cultists stand upon the infernal surface, smelled their roasting meat, heard their matchless silence in the face of it all.

The knight's gaze lingered on the black bones. "Your people are driven to madness," he said. "Your fires consume you."

"And yours as well, ser knight. Not all of these bones are my kin."

"Corrupted regardless. Through want of power."

"Or something they found beautiful, perhaps. Have you ever lost yourself in the fire's dance?"

The knight did not respond, instead driving his foot through a nearby skull, sparks billowing like wind-swept pollen. "You would defend these savages you've conscripted me to kill?"

"I do not condemn their ways. I am simply meeting these people with a language that they understand. They make their worlds through annihilation, so that is how I will answer them. Your invasion showed me this."

* * *

They saw us coming and with crazed hands they hurled their magics at us, black smoke cutting a curling trail through the sky as the flames arced, descended, splashed against the knight's raised shield.

The man's face blanched and he turned to me with bulging eyes, "I thought you said you would protect me!"

Another streak of flame approached, but with my hand I turned it aside before it could reach us; it shattered into a nearby tree with the force of the mountain, the limbs exploding into shrapnel. Crazed and powerful, the cultists' fire, but often directionless, easily curtailed and redirected. I showed the knight my confident smile.

"I wanted you to feel the stakes. Now come, cut our passage through these men. I will turn away their flames."

We ascended into their camp: fire-baked shelters made with clay hauled from the river at the base of the mountain; threadbare clothes strung on a hemp line; cauldrons bubbling, the flesh of their dead turning on spits, the fat popping. A sickening place, but their home nonetheless, and I felt for them even as I brought their revelation.

In my previous attempts to reach the summit, the cultists' number proved too many, my own aging skills incapable of fending off the horde. But with the knight they broke upon us like water on rock, and we carved through their bodies with ease.

In between my own magical workings, the knight and his tarnished plate moved with a blunt-edged grace. His ferocity held my gaze, and I felt I stood before a work of art with every cut and thrust. Throats opened at his command, organs popped, blood sprayed until we sludged through red mud. A wild cultist, frustrated as his flames extinguished beneath the force of my might, bellowed a challenge and rushed, muscle-braided arms outstretched and clasping. The knight caught the brunt against his shield, sliding through the blood until he readjusted, planted his feet, rooted. With a grunt, he shoved the man back and slid his sword up to the hilt into his chest. While they grappled, I dispatched another of the assailants, a thin-limbed man looking to catch the knight unawares; with a whisper I boiled his brains until they leaked from his ears.

Against the two of us, the cultists could not hope to halt our progress.

* * *

The summit yawned before us. Covered in blood, the pair of us, enshrouded in smoke, blisters forming on our skin from the heat: we stood, finally, at the end.

Beneath my feet, in the earth, the mountain churned and spewed its guts. Around us the lava streams flowed in mighty blazing rivers, some branching into small tributaries, allowing us to navigate to the crater-mouth top.

"Go on and end it then, sorcerer," the knight gasped, breathless from the bloodletting, the climb, the inferno. He knelt on the rocky ground. "Let us be done with this."

I knelt beside him and pressed my palms against the steaming rock. My mate's words returned to me: *Use this man. Close the mountain. Sew close the tear in our home.*

Heat rippled up and out and around as I sent myself into the rock, descending toward the frothing fire. The skin on my hands blackened and cracked. Something seared itself behind my eyes, and a pressure built like a pressing stone.

I knew, within a moment, the task was beyond my abilities.

Withdrawing, I cradled my hands in my lap, tried to staunch the bleeding.

"Well," the knight demanded, his armor screeching as he turned to me. "Is it done?"

I looked at him, and we held the mountain and smoke and fire between us, and I confessed. "The task is not done, ser knight. Too great, the wound. I cannot close it. You have my apologies."

The knight attempted to stand, stumbled and coughed from the smoke, then rose again. His eyes flared in the lava's light. "I don't want your apologies. I killed those people so you could trudge up your blasted mountain, all the while against my will. You compelled me with your burning sorceries, and now you tell me it cannot be done? I say you lie."

I stood to meet him, and as I moved a piece of our perch broke free and slid into the summit-mouth, the lake of fire swallowing it with a hiss.

"We both killed those men, and now we learn their deaths served no purpose. We will burn their bodies on the way down. This mountain will continue to bring forth its death and tarnish my home. My children will grow in the shadow of smoke, and you will continue your wandering."

Abruptly I turned and began to retrace our path, placing my feet with care. If the knight spoke against the mountain's fire, I could not hear a word, but I felt his trembling steps follow in my wake

Diary of The Wolf

By Adam McPhee

But keep the wolf far thence, that's foe to men,

For with his nails he'll dig them up again.

— John Webster, *The White Devil*

March 1, 1660[1]: walked about all day, hoping perchance to meet upon my cozen Richard, that we might go over the business of the last full moon and the fits of wolfing that did overtake us, which worries me greatly, I having been sore vexed

---

1 1659/1660 O.S./N.S. dates. England did not switch from the Julian to the Gregorian calendar until the 1750s. In England, Queen Elizabeth I and her privy council had looked favourably to a Gregorian-like royal commission recommendation to drop 10 days from the calendar but the virulent opposition of the Anglican bishops, who argued that the Pope was undoubtedly the fourth great beast of Daniel, led the Queen to let the matter be quietly dropped. — A.M.

of late by dreams of the foulest mongrel knavery and so do fear me the worst.

Did find him at his tailor's with his sister Anne, and we three of us off to the Globe to broach a vessel of ale and discuss matters of the wolfing disease. Richard did say that he remembered it a miserable occasion, the worst fit in his seven years of it, and that he recalled digging up a great hole on Hampstead heath with my assistance, and therein burying the bones of some poor rascal we must have troubled upon. I did tell him about my vexing dreams and together we surmised it must have been the butcher, Vincent, who had been hounding Richard over a bill of 18L. Neither of us seeing him since, we did soon fear the worst and did not dare go to check upon his shop lest we be recognized, and so sent Anne in our stead to see if he is alive or no, she being less likely to attract suspicion and altogether less troublesome in her fits. We tarried late waiting for Anne's report, quenching our thirst with a pot of ale and tasting sweet meats. Then I home to bed still much troubled by a fit which is now almost a fortnight past.

March 2: all the day within doors to do a good deale of work upon a remedy chanced upon in a manual of instruction against witchcraft and dis-ease. The heat this Galenical produced in my stomach gathered the sediments of my water into a slime, though I fear this concoction shall prove as useless as mass-going and all other remedies.

March 3: To the coffeehouse listening to learned gentlemen debate whether we should have a king again or no, and by what condition, if any, and by turns slowly I wondered whether a king on the throne would reduce my fitting by the pleasure of God, but I dare not speak it and so keep quiet until Richard should arrive, and we off then to the Dolphin, which serves us palpable beef and Lambeth ale, he much anxious but it being too crowded for free discourse on matters of the moon. Then out in the street he says my she-cozen Anne did not return from her errand to the butcher's and he worries greatly for her.

Home with Richard despite my wife's misgivings, it being too dark to search Anne out. Much talk of his longer experience of wolfing upon the continent and his desire to return there. He did drink about a quart of wine by his own account and me also. Then at our viols to put my wife at ease, though we made but mean music, Richard's heart vexed by his missing sister.

March 4: My head aching mightily I awakened against my will at Dawn, as Richard was keen to begin our hunt, though I take him first to Wilkinson's for a morning draught and some cakes. We stamped about the streets in search of Anne, then parted ways as to search more ground. I to the Shambles in Newgate Market and skulked about until I saw Vincent the butcher who spoke to me kindly and with complete ignorance of any wolfing, and by my guilt I was persuaded to buy a good goose. Now vexed mighty sore wondering who we buried.

Thence to Mother Lams wherein I chanced to sit by Crocutus and Tullia. Four or five pints of wine and a barrel of oysters with them, both very excited, for they had with them John Porta's Natural Magick in XX Books, which tells how living creatures of divers kinds may be mingled and coupled together, that from them, new and yet profitable kinds of living Creatures may be generated. Crocutus says it shows his ancient line, for there is a chapter which tells of the Chaonides, a line of wolves gendered from a kind of wolf called Chaos. We could find nothing in this tome about witches, and so it is of no profit to me. Tullia did tell me she had been to St Paul's Churchyarde to have the Porta clasped and bossed, and there saw Richard and Anne, who seemed well.

March 5: My poor wife all day at the goose and other good things, of which I am highly pleased. I to Unthanke's to retrieve the ferrandin ripped and torn from my last wolfing.

Thence home and there comes Richard and Anne and my conceited brother, John, to play at cards and to sup with us. I had for them tanzy and neats' tongues, then the good goose, and then fruit and cheese and a tart. Such good cheer was had that I did not mind John's aggravations and prying, and did share again the story of how I first came to wolfing, when I became lost crossing the fens on my return from that business with Mallorie the Scot, and was overcome by such a hunger that I surrendered to my temptation, and so did steal a fragrant mince-pie from the sill of a meek dwelling. I am no subtle man, and did prance from that place too gleefully, and did burn my hands by its heat, and so dropped the mince and uttered a cry, and thus I was discovered by the were-woman who claims descent from Atla, who confounded me with blasphemies for many days (and though I dare not say it, the debauched hag against my will did baiser moi et faire l'autre thing in las tenebras so as to make mi mismo espender but with no pleasure), and she did call upon the worms of the earth to curse me to become a wolf with the moon, and it was only by my meeting later of Richard and Anne and the others that I have not despaired overmuch.

When John leaves, Richard tells me to-morrow he will see Mr Pargiter the goldsmith, for payment of the fine stuff we brought him after our last spree, Pargiter now having had time to profit by it.

March 7 (Ash Wednesday): Lay long in bed, and by and by discoursed with my wife the problem of the coming moon, and how I might not do her nor anyone any hurt, and together we questioned who might be buried in the heath.

Thence to Wotton's, the shoemaker, where I gave him a good cheese for his lent and purchased some buckles 20S to be put on my shoes after the moon, and he did tell me he would be glad to have a king again, if only that the theatres might be open.

To church in the afternoon, that God might take pity on my wolfing, but did not take heed of the sermon and feare it does no good.

Then outside St James I find Mr Pearse the surgeon, who does take an interest in my disease, and he introduces me to his friend, Samuel Pepys, whom I find to be courteous but still a very conceited man, and who Mr Pearse tells us may soon be going overseas with the navy to treat with Charles Stuart to be our king. Mr Pearse bid me try the seeds of the sensitive plant, which do curle when touched. Mr Pepys, guessing at my affliction, said at Pope's Head Alley I might look for Adam Chard's shop, who does sell little devices of protection against wolfing. Mr Pearse then swears Mr Pepys to all secrecy on this matter.

March 8: Up betimes, and Richard comes with news that that Rogue Mr Pargiter did cheat us, sharing only 5L for all the goodes and wares we did bring him.

When I tell him of the coming restoration of the king he gets all afright, and reminds me that our kind did not have a good time of it with the last King Charles, or before him with King James, who made wolfing known in his Daemonologie, calling us 'war-woolfes' and 'men-woolfes,' and set out to silence our barking. I rebut him and say we have been no more comfortable under the Protector, and he sayes I am too young to remember the witch trials and bid me remember what Mallorie told us of Berwick, but I tell him I am no friend of witches, for it was a witch that made me a wolf. All in all a bad time to fall to quarrelling, for the moon is up soon, and we with preparations still to make, so we hold to an uneasy truce and I finish my accounts and bid good-bye to my poor wife and set out with Richard.

March 10 [continued from March 8]: To Pope's Head Alley and find Adam Chard's shoppe to purchase the device against wolfing, but find Mr Pepys means only catcalls, toy pipes for jeering players on the stage, and so of no use.

Then find the officers of the Army making a horrible din, remonstrating against Charles Stuart and anyone else who might rule over us. It seems a bad omen and we to Three Tuns Tavern but find the wine do not calm us. We think of going by coach or by water away from London, as is our custom for the moon, but it is late in the day and all arrangements fail us. Anne arrives with leashes but we with no more kennel or dogge-house are like to be stoned or murdered should we use them. The day growing long without resolve, we become haunted with the memory of Venner's men saying we were the millennium and chasing us about with axes.

Richard desires to pay John Pargiter a visit and bark and bite at him for his cheating us, but I make him vow to do no violence except that which the wolfes make us do. I out to the alley to piss mighty hard, and returning find my way blocked by a wolfe with a slobbering tongue dripping drool like a great mastiffe dog but bigger. By his periwigg and his frock and his band I see it is Richard, and I help him take these off so he can go on all foures as is wont of a wolf, and I see Anne is changed too but by means of her fangs and her claws does not need my aid, and now I am changed and the houre of the wolf do come and we runne one after another in the street and we do what what our nature tell us and we make our awwooouus, our wolfe howls, and we scare any folk who meet us and we vex any man who greet us.

In the morning we come back into our selfes and find each other smattered in deer's blood and lolling on Hampstead heath. Anne with her garments all missing and asunder, and I worry I will sin now worse than in the night, but no, Richard remembers the hole we dug and what's in it, the meat from the butcher's we robbed during last month's moon, but also other good things for when we wake, clothes and shoes and a few small coins, things we are all lacking now. It does my heart good to know there is no murder this month.

For me the wolfing is still a dream that I do not believe on waking, but Richard says this will pass and I will come to remember more of it and when I do I will have more sense of the wolf and will not be so frightened and will be more of myself during the moon.

The mutton is no good and besides it is lent, but there is a cheese and bottles of wine which restore us some, then we dress and find there is not enough for a coach, so we put on shoes and trudge wearily back to the city. When we are almost there we find Crocutus and Tullia and they hear our story and take us to "The Bottle of Hay," in St. John's Street, to have pasties and broach a vessel of ale. Crocutus relates how they joined us in the night, and how I scented a pair of drunkards and we all of us hounded them from their tavern down to the Thames and thence to Axe Yard, but there our fortune shifted and for many hours these drunks did taunt us and tease us from a high place, blowing upon catcalls, which drove us mad with a fury we could not sate, and hurling stones at us.[2] And only after a time did we leave them for other ventures.

Soon I am home again and greet my wife merrily but also with sadness for this disease does harry and torment us. And so to bed, and to a fitful and restless sleep wherein I am troubled by dreams of mongrel things, but then a good sleep,

---

2 A later entry confirms their victim is Samuel Pepys and his friend Mr Butler. Pepys makes no mention of this incident in his more famous diary, though he did spend the evening with Mr Butler (aka Monsieur L'Impertinent) and on the day after the attack he swears off alcohol for a time, writing, "All night troubled in my thoughts … I could not sleep, and being overheated with drink I made a promise the next morning to drink no strong drink this week, for I find that it makes me sweat and puts me quite out of order." — A.M.

untroubled, and when I wake it almost evening again, and my wife has a cod's head and a soup made of pease for my supper.

March 11: All day at my leisure, reading Caxton's The Right Pleasant And Goodly History Of The Foure Sonnes Of Aymon. I laugh when Renaud kills the cobbler who knows him and would betray him to Charlemagne for money, but my wife calls it a very sad scene on account of the presence of the cobbler's widow and orphans and by turns I see she is right.

March 12: At the Star in Cheapside and Richard is all put out, saying he and Anne will sell all their property at the Exchange and then depart across the Channell for France with great haste. When I press him for his reasons he confesses that two of our wolf-cozens were taken alive at the last moon, and are being held in a kennel constructed anew at the Exchange, and are to be taken to the old bear-garden to be baited against whatever fierce creatures are to be had. My soul is struck with horror at Richard's story. There has been no baiting in all the time of mine and Richard's wolfing, or almost none, for it was banned. But now it seems there is one more horror to add to our litany.

Then to Mr Shott the woodmonger to arrange for some firing against to-morrow.

March 13: With Richard to the Exchange to view with great pity our captive cozens. In the kennel is one man, much in need of shaving, and alongside him one wolf. They are roughly handled by Monck's soldiers, who abuse the man greatly by making him do dog-tricks and gnaw upon a bone. Richard made the sign by which we know each other to be cozens, and though the captive was the focus of all attention, our cozen returned our sign. And so by subtlety we inquired how his friend did not change back with the moon, and by signs we come to believe it to do with the strange esterminal stone on the wolf's collar. It is a great pity to see.

It rains a good deal and this matches the sadness of our mood. Richard has not the heart to sell his goods. We hear too that the King of Sweden is newly dead, but what care do we have for him when he is so far away and our hearts are already so full of grief?

March 14: Crocutus sends Tullia to me at the coffee house, and we trod through the hardest rain to meet him at St James', and with him James Pearse the surgeon, who tells me our captive cozen might be baited at the old Cock-Pit at Whitehall, which was shuttered when plays were banned. If not there then the

Beargarden. Mr Pearse worries that if the soldiers bait a man, even one known to wolf with the moon, then the Fanatiques will set off like so much powder, and so he resolves to help us free our kin, though it be parilous and we putting our necks at risk.

At home my wife has herring and eggs. As we sup I tell her of Pearse's proposal, and how by and by I do have some sympathy for the Fanatiques, that it is right to be outraged at cruelty, but all the same we are often misguided and led astray. I put it in my mind that if our work goes well I will let my wife have the servant she has long wanted for but which we could not much afford, and also to set aside my affairs so that if the worst should come to me then she is not so badly off.

March 15: Up betimes and soon to the Exchange, where a proud painter with his brush and on his ladder washed out the inscription calling the old king a tyrant. The soldiers there look to arrange a baiting, but so far everyone balks. I find they are released from Monck's army some weeks ago, and are in fact now a traineband militia, though it makes no difference to me what they are. Any man who keeps his fellow man in a dogge-kennel is but a demon in masquerade. Then there is a great bonfire in the exchange, and people right jolly, and begin calling out for King Charles II as if he were already with us.

Thence resolve to find Richard and Anne and bring them into our plot, but they not home and so I about the streets to look for them.

Then alone to an ordinary I do not know, and it being Lent the man will not serve me a pullet, and so but a dirty dinner.

All the talk is filled with rumours of the officers of the army and their discontent, that they might make a stir or try some new thing. The Parliament sits late into the night, and do not dissolve themselves, and so I wonder if they are about some new thing, too.

And so home, and to bed.

March 16: Today the Parliament dissolved itself at long last, and there are to be elections in a month's time, and Charles II Stuart to come as our king.

Quickly to the Reindeer to avoid the rain, it being a tavern where we are not known and can speak freely by dint of the general noise, and I relay all that Mr Pearse and Crocotus have to say about our kennelled compatriots.

Richard is still for going to the continent, and tells me I should come, with my wife or no. And Crocotus and Tullia too, if they wish it. We'll straight to Paris to see his Huguenot relations, both of blood and of wolfing. Yet in Paris we are guaranteed no more safety than in London, and it is unknown to us. He agrees, and tells me we will stay only a short time there, in order to prepare for a journey very far afield. Then Richard tells us of Pulican, who he would have us seek out, who is the master of all our kind, and lives far away in Armenia, where he is a sheepdog to flocks of good folk and a wolf to flocks of bad folk. I have never heard of Pulican and press Richard for detail, though Richard isn't sure if Pulican is like us at the moon, or if at all hours he is a wolf, or if he is a giant, or mayhap a cynocephalic, or a wolf who walks like a man. At this my risen hopes are dashed back down again. I have seen many strange things since the witch cursed me, but the strange things I have heard are so often twisted by rumour and man's desiring that when I finally chance to see them they are not at all as I was told.

I can see in his face Richard is uncertain too.

And so then Anne speaks, saying she would like to help us free our brethren, both because it is right to do and because she is curious about the esterminal which seems to keep one of the two captives a wolf, regardless of the calendar. By and by Richard sees that he cannot let his sister Anne do this thing by herself, forgetting that we already have our numbers, and so he resolves to join us too.

Thence to St James's to tell Mr Pearse he can count two more to our planning, and hear from him that the butchers propose baiting our fellows against a most vicious bull of theirs that has killed two horses and the boy riding upon one of them. The traineband men mull it over and put off any commitment, for they prefer a bear but there is none to be had in all of London just now.

And so home, and worried, and a dish of cabbage and mustards and vinegar, and with it a quart of cider.

March 17: From Crocutus we hear that the traineband men accept the butchers' offer and the baiting is to take place three days hence. Mr Pearse to try and have Monck put a stop to it, but we fear it will do no good.

March 18: All day putting things in order for my wife lest anything should happen to me, and still I feel it does me no good. So at last I retire from it, knowing there is no more I can do, but to focus on doing this thing to free our fellows, even if it should make us look like bandits and cost us our good names or even our lives.

Stopping at an alehouse on Drury Lane looking for Mr Pearse but find instead Mr Pepys. He is sore vexed at something I don't understand and though I'm not of his party he keeps calling over asking if I have skinned any cats of late and finally I ask what he means and he produces the catcall from Mr Chard's shop in Pope's Head Alley, telling me that on the night of the moon some of my fellows gave him hell. I apologize and tell him what little I remember and know of it, and Mr Pepys admits he was with his friend Mr Butler, both quite overcome with drink, and Mr Butler insisting on antagonizing us. And so we make peace between us. It seems Mr Pepys is shortly going to sea and so, like me, he is trying to get his accounts in order. Without much thought I mention that I keep this diary and the value it has provided in such matters, and his eyes alight and he asks me a great many questions, mostly on the theme of how I keep it hidden, given the difficulties it would cause me if my affliction should become publick knowledge. Finally he gives me some advice on finding Mr Pearse at this hour, but it being late I finish my ale and toasted cakes and return home instead and put my things there in a little order. And so, to bed.

March 19: Up, and after a morning draught, with my wife to the Exchange, where I see Crocutus and Tullia about, but pretend not to know them. The talk is giddy and in favour of the return of the king, and few speak against it. Then making as if to buy good things for my wife, I discern that the baiting is to happen to-morrow, at the old Beargarden.

At the Dolphin, we meet Richard and Anne and Mr Pearse, and come to agreement that our ambush would be best placed along the road from the Exchange to the garden before the traineband is to cross the Thames. Richard and Anne are sent to espy the ground and find a place for us to lay in wait, while Tullia shows my wife and I some masques she has made for us from sackcloth so that our faces should not be known. Mr Pearse promises us his pistol and plenty of powder, and Crocutus and I will each bring ours as well.

Thence home by coach through the rain and the wind.

March 20: Up betimes and a great feeling of worry in my wife and I, this day being the day of the ambush. I ask her to pray for our success and leave for my morning draught, then by coach to meet our fellows.

From the beginning there are problems. Mr Pearse is unable to come, we know not why. The weather so windy and damp and the rain so frequent, we reason his powder is no great loss and we five set off for the ambuscade, but here again find trouble, as the rain floods the streets, and some rogues for a laugh row their boats up King Street, and the wind is high and the tide great. It is a struggle just to travel into the city, and we decide to send Anne and Tullia home, but they will not.

Soon we cannot help but laugh, grave danger or no, for the weather turns our effort into a giddy farce. At a tavern to warm our selves with ale and hear the boat the Maidenhead is cast away, and we jest on the theme that the Maidenhead is lost, though our laughter dies and our wits return when we hear there are twelve souls aboard her, now lost.

We resolve to go to the Exchange and free our kin if we can, on the assumption that the baiting is put off for the day, but find the insolent and prideful fools of the traineband on the street in procession. Crocutus is for attacking straightaway, though the traineband men number at least fifteen, more if their draymen join the fray, and large crowds gather to watch despite the rain, and the crowds would surely not take our side. Richard advises caution, and we see he is right, and we seek out our inner wolves, to stalk and wait for chances as they do.

Soon the traineband procession meets the butchers' procession and we worry we have lost our chance with so many men about. The butchers' great bull is angry and cruel and it takes four men to pull the ropes about his neck and a fifth to hold a chain tied to his hind leg. He snorts hot breath and no one dares approach him. We are thinking of turning back when the dray holding our compatriots becomes stuck in the road and the folk get rowdy as the traineband men frustrate themselves attempting to unstuck their conveyance.

I would put on my masque but Richard motions against it and instead I follow him to the dray on false pretense of helping the draymen. I can see the lock on the kennel will not be opened but the bars are only wood, and I think they might break. No one stops me from putting my hand on or in this cage. The esterminal on the wolf's collar is a brilliant green against this cloudy, grey city and I cannot look away and I reach out because I must touch it I must hold it I must see what it can do and now I am a wolf though there is no moon.

Now the crowd goes from rowdy to panicked because there is a wolf among them and I show no love to these traineband men. I growl and I bark and I bite. I am too fast for their swords and their shot and no man can catch me and I dodge any who would block my way. Now I attack the butchers not to do any great hurt to them, but to scare those controlling the bull. The bull fears me and would gore me with his sharp horns but he hates his captors with the fire of hell and now he is free and there is a great commotion indeed.

Anne and Tullia have on their masques and hack against the kennel with butchers' knives. Crocutus levels his gun and another at the traineband men but they do not fire on account of the damp. Yet the traineband fire their guns without problem or hesitation and a stray shot sets Richard's periwig alight and I told him to take it off before we entered the fray but he is a vain man at all times, and so he takes it off and cursing, throws it to the ground.

Now our compatriots are free but the one who is an over-hairy man is shot and falls from the dray and slumps face-down in the street. Thence Crocutus is stabbed by a butcher and drops his weapons and we do not know how we are going to flee, as the traineband's dray cuts off one end of the street and the bull gores anyone who goes against the other end. Then the new wolf licks at Crocutus until Crocutus touches the esterminal and now he too is a wolf and one-by-one Anne and Tullia and Richard are wolves too. I bite at a traineband soldier who is passing out their case of pistols, but find his harness is lined with iron. No matter. Richard calls us all together and we know it is time to flee, and the traineband and the butchers and the passersby are inclined to let us go.

We howl and vaunt and run wild through London. The rain is no impediment to our peregrinations, and feels good and cooling on our thick coats.

At the Moorefields we stop and the new wolf agitates, wanting to lick the esterminal, but he cannot on account of its placement on his collar, but then Richard licks it and goes into himself again and removes the collar and before long we all come back into ourselves. It is strange but unlike with the moon we have not had to abandon our garments, and they are fixed upon us now. The new wolf is a Scot named James and I ask if he knows Mallory and he laughs and says no, but then cries for the loss of his friend and resolves to tell us all about their wolfing and their esterminal stone and how they were captured, but first we must help Crocutus, who is sore wounded but only as a man. Still, we are all of us happy to have a new cozen.

So we back to wolfing and more stalky this time, for we must return to town and find Mr Pearse, who is a surgeon of wounds and has helped us before, and has always kept our secret, and especially that of Crocutus, who being a highborn man has farther to fall. This done, Mr Pearse tells us to lay low for a time, and he will enquire if we are to be hunted out, and my wife is pleasantly surprised to find me home unhurt and at so early an hour.

March 21: Against a very strong wind to the Star in Cheapside, and after four or five pints of wine comes Richard and our new friend James. James tells us his father was known to wolf, and when he died James inherited the curse. His friend Thomas, murdered yesterday by traineband men, was the only other wolf James knew, and they both deserters of Cromwell's army after sacking Wexford, which he did say was a most terrible crime and which troubled him more than anything he had yet done under the moon. Thomas had heard of the esterminal while in the New Model Army, when he had gone with his captain to deliver some books to Oxford for safekeeping. Among these was the diary of John Dee, who in his time had been horoscopist for Queen Elizabeth. Dee wrote of keeping the esterminal for protection against wolves, and had it buried with him. Finding Dee's body proved a great difficulty for James and Thomas, as the famed alchemist died a pauper. Their months of grave robbing in Mortlake did bring them to the notice of the traineband men, who captured them and brought them to the city for baiting.

Then comes Anne, who tells us Tullia will not leave Crocutus's side, for though his wound is well-mended the injury of it may yet kill him. I propose to go and see him, but

Anne says I dare not go, for a man claiming to be the Royal Lymerer[3] comes saying he is rounding up stray hunting dogs and Anne says from the look he gives her he seems to know what we are. We know he is not who he says, for there is no king yet to appoint him. So here comes our new trouble, and Richard says if the man persists we must use the esterminal stone so that we may wolf and hunt him by scent, and James promises the esterminal will forever be made ready to us, and we promise to be a good friend to James, just as Richard and Anne once promised to be a good friend to me in my wolfing, and to this day they have kept to it true.

And so home, and to bed.

March 23: My wife and I lay late in bed in the morning and I confess it feels as if we are at the end of some thing, some interregnum, where before there was only my life and hers, and then comes the wolfing curse and all the chaos it has sown against us and now at least our ignorance of it comes to an end, and so now if God be pleased we may be restored to some sensible life, that though I still be wolfing at the moon now I at

---

3 One who controls a lymer, or lyme-hound, 'lyme' meaning leash. Montague Summers' commentary notes the term would have been suspiciously archaic-sounding even in 1660. — A.M.

last have some knowledge of it, and some cozens I can rely upon for these things I do not yet know.

And then up, and she reminds me I have new buckles still to put on my shoes, and many small things to accomplish, and they may yet add up to a great thing, and to a contented life.

Tales from the Magician's Skull, Issue 11

reviewed by Robin Marx

Tales From The Magician's Skull No. 11 collects eight new sword and sorcery stories curated by Howard Andrew Jones. It features cover artwork by fantasy paperback master Sanjulian, and each story is illustrated by artists, including Jason Edwards, Tom Galambos, and Stefan Poag.

"Test of the Runeweavers," by H. T. Grossen, receives the cover treatment for this issue. Young Frode, a member of the Viking-inspired Aegirvarg people, embarks on his first ocean voyage as an apprentice *runerikr*, or wielder of spoken rune-based magic. Investigating mysterious coastal raids, Frode and his fellows encounter strangers from a far-off land with their own potent ideograph-based magic. This brisk story covers a great deal of territory despite its slim page count, and the rune magic feels flashy and novel.

"Lady of the Frost" is the latest Shintaro Oba tale by C. L. Werner, a name that should be familiar to fans of *Warhammer* and Games Workshop's Black Library imprint. As with previous installments, wandering samurai Oba comes into conflict with a supernatural threat from Japanese folklore. "Lady of the Frost" is a solid example of sword and sorcery adventure in an underrepresented setting.

Trespassing in temples devoted to bizarre and malign gods is a common (and exciting!) trope in sword & sorcery, but if this issue has a flaw, it's the inclusion of three such stories in a single installment. Bill Pearce's "The Eyes of Rath Kanon" is the first of this issue's unadvertised evil temple trilogy. The twisty plot and shifting loyalties intrigued, but despite a strong start and conclusion it felt like the middle portion of this contribution lacked the propulsive momentum found in the other stories.

"Ghostwise" by Caias Ward was the highlight of the issue, and a story I suspect *Old Moon Quarterly* readers are especially predisposed to enjoy. Dark-skinned but with chalk-white hands, gun-slinging mystic Obba Babatunde is summoned to a king's court to attend to a haunted princess with identical markings. Like Obba himself, Princess Jansynth exists simultaneously in both the realms of the living and the dead, making her vulnerable to constant ghostly attacks unless she can build up her own defenses. As she struggles to keep her soul intact, Jansynth learns a devastating truth about her spectral tormentor and her own heritage. Cleverly plotted, "Ghostwise" reminds me of the early *Witcher* short stories by Andrzej

Sapkowski, where the true monster isn't always obvious at first glance. Ward's hero and his talents are worthy of further elaboration, and I hope to see more Obba stories in the future.

Set in Earth in ancient times rather than a secondary world, Mark Mellon's "Melkart and the Whore of Babylon" masterfully transforms antiquity into a lush and decadent sword and sorcery setting. Envious of her influence on Babylon's populace, King Belshazzar plots to use a religious ceremony as cover and assassinate Inanna, the priestess of Ishtar, replacing both her and the goddess she serves with a more amenable sect. Unwilling to participate in such a dastardly scheme, Belshazzar's hired sword Melkart immediately reveals the conspiracy to Inanna, offering himself as her protector at great personal risk. Just as the odds seem insurmountable, "Melkart and the Whore of Babylon" concludes with a truly epic finale.

Dawn Vogel's "Kick in the Door and Improvise" distinguishes itself from the other stories by virtue of its humor. Unable to infiltrate a castle due to the bright moon overhead, two thieves hired to steal a king's crown seek magical assistance. A sorcerer offers to dim the moon to hide their approach, provided they can collect all the ingredients required for the spell on a tight schedule. The final heist itself ends up almost an afterthought; most of the story concerns itself with the hunt for an elusive black pearl. The wry, freewheeling tone and focus on spell components pleasantly reminded me of the *Dungeons & Dragons: Honor Among Thieves* film, and the story offered a refreshing change of pace from the uniformly serious tales composing the rest of the issue.

In "The Lens of Being," by Daniel Amatiello, a pirate queen stumbles across a menacing cult lurking in a cliff-side temple complex on the coast of India. While the heretical Buddhist sect featured in the story had great potential, its aims and methods felt underdeveloped and the climactic monster too familiar. Not a bad story, but it suffers by appearing alongside two other temple raid stories.

The issue ends on a particularly strong note with "Bound in Brass and Iron," by Matthew X. Gomez. When partially devoured bodies start turning up at the scene of a newly constructed temple, Liam the Black is hired to investigate. The trail leads him into a deeper temple, where a forgotten demon strains against its binding. This is the best of the issue's unofficial evil temple trilogy, with a resourceful hero, fascinating spellcraft, and tense action.

Each issue of *Tales From The Magician's Skull* concludes with a brief appendix called "The Monster Pit," featuring game statistics of the monsters appearing in the various stories for use with publisher Goodman Games' *Dungeon Crawl Classics* role-playing game. It's a gimmick, but a fun one that hopefully encourages tabletop gamers to engage more with the literary roots of their hobby.

Since launching in 2018, *Tales From The Magician's Skull* quickly established itself as a quality venue for fantasy tales written in the pulp adventure tradition, and both the fiction and the artwork in this issue maintains that high level of excellence. *Tales From The Magician's Skull* benefits from a tight focus on sword and sorcery, making it a one-stop venue for fast-paced fantasy action.

About the Authors

R.H. Berry is a Canadian author of fantasy and horror, with short stories and poetry in a variety of publications. His website is www.theirritablequeer.com.

J.M. Hayes is a writer fascinated by folklore, mythology, theology, and mysticism, and all those things that lie between them. Having read Theology at Bangor University for his undergraduate, he went on to undertake a postgraduate in Museum Studies at the University of Leicester. He is also the author of "The Riddle of Shurá", which was published in the Winter 2013 edition of *Luvah: Journal of the Creative Imagination*. He currently lives on an old farm amidst the wooded hills of Huntingdonshire, England.

Matt Holder teaches rhetoric and composition in the St. Louis area. His academic writing can be found in *Disability Studies Quarterly* and *ImageTexT*, his reviews in *Strange Horizons* and *Spiral Tower Press*, and his fiction in *Old Moon Quarterly* and other indie presses that have since folded. He lives in Fenton, MO, with his wife, Maggie, and their dog, Lily.

Adam McPhee is a Canadian writer whose work has appeared in *Wyngraf*, *Dark Moon Digest*, *Ahoy Comics*, and elsewhere. He can be found on twitter @ChalicothereX, and has recently launched a substack newsletter, *Adam's Notes*. He lives in Alberta.

Katherine Quevedo was born and raised near Portland, Oregon, where she works as an analyst and lives with her husband and two sons. Her poetry has been nominated for the Pushcart Prize and the Rhysling Award and has appeared in *Asimov's*, *Heroic Fantasy Quarterly*, *Anterior Skies*, *TOWER Magazine*, and elsewhere. Find her at www.katherinequevedo.com.

In 1977, **Dariel R. A. Quiogue** was simultaneously exposed to Star Wars, Herodotus, Homer, Edgar Rice Burroughs, and Robert E. Howard, and his brain has never been the same since. He now writes F&SF in his spare time, flavored by his fascination for history, science, the sea, and the richness and diversity of Asian cultures. His creative motto is "simple stories, powerfully told."

A professional author since 2007, **Josh Reynolds** has over thirty novels to his name, as well as numerous short stories, novellas and audio scripts. Born and raised in South Carolina, he now resides in Sheffield with his wife and daughter, as well as a highly excitable dog and something he hopes is a cat. A complete list of his work can be found at https://joshuamreynolds.co.uk/.

R.L. Summerling is a writer from South East London. In her free time she enjoys befriending crows in Nunhead Cemetery. She has stories in *Maudlin House, Seize The Press, Interzone, Northern Gravy* and more. She is the author of the micro collection *FLESHPOTS* which is available for free on itch.io. You can find her at rlsummerling.com and on Twitter, Instagram and Bluesky as @RLSummerling.

19074187R00080